Preface.

Lest the account given in this book of the "trekking" springbucks should be considered an exaggeration, it may be mentioned that in 1892, when the author held the appointments of Civil Commissioner for Namaqualand and Special Magistrate for the Northern Border of the Cape Colony, he was obliged to issue a hundred stand of Government arms to the Boers for the purpose of driving back the game which threatened to overrun those parts of Namaqualand where ground is cultivated. As it was, there was some difficulty in repelling the invasion.

The term "Bushman," strictly speaking, only applies to the diminutive former inhabitants of the Desert, who are now practically extinct to the south of the Orange River. The Trek-Boer, however, usually calls every Hottentot of low stature a Bushman.

Chapter One.

The Land of the Trek-Boer.

Immediately to the south of the great Orange River for three hundred arid miles of its course before it sinks through the thirsty sands, or spooms in resistless torrent into the Atlantic Ocean, lies a region of which little is known, in which dwell people unlike any others in South Africa, or possibly in the world.

This region is known as Bushmanland—the name having reference to its former inhabitants who, proving themselves "unfit," were abolished from the face of the earth. Bushmanland is at present intermittently inhabited by a nomadic population of Europeans of Dutch descent, who are known as "Trek-Boers." To "trek" means, literally, to "pull," but its colloquial significance is—to move about from place to place.

The Trek-Boers are, so to say, poor relations of the sturdy Dutchmen who have done so much towards reclaiming South Africa from savagery. The conditions under which they live are not favourable to moral or physical improvement.

These people are dwellers in tents and beehive-shaped structures known as "mat-houses," a form of architecture adopted from the Hottentots. The latter are constructed of large mats made of rushes strung upon strands of bark or other vegetable fibre, and are stretched over wattles stuck by the larger end into the ground in a circle, the diameter of which may vary from fifteen to twenty-five feet, and which have the thin ends drawn down over each other until a dome is formed. Such structures are lighter and more portable than the lodges of the North American Indians—in fact one may easily be erected and pulled down within five minutes. Strange to say they are almost completely water-tight.

A wagon and a couple of tents or mat-houses constitutes the camp and castle of the Trek-Boer. He has never known anything else in the shape of a dwelling; it satisfies all his architectural aspirations, it fulfils his ideal of comfort in a tenement, and he harbours contempt for any structure which cannot be moved about to suit the convenience or caprice of its owner.

The Trek-Boer owns no land. He wanders with his flocks and herds over the vast, unsurveyed tract which is all the world to him, following the uncertain courses of thunderstorms which happen to have been deflected from their ordinary beat and strayed across the desert. The rain from these intermittently fills the shallow, cup-like depressions in the underlying rock with water. Such depressions are invariably choked with sand, but by digging at certain known spots a scanty supply of water may sometimes be obtained.

The Trek-Boer occasionally becomes rich in flocks and herds, but every eight or ten years the inevitable drought occurs. Then his stock dies off from thirst and starvation, and he has to begin the world again, a poor man.

The Trek-Boer is a being *sui generis*. He is usually ignorant to a degree unknown among men called civilised. He is untruthful, prejudiced, superstitious, cunning, lazy, and dirty. On the other hand he is extremely hospitable. Simple as a child in many things, and as trusting where his confidence has once been given, he cannot be known without being loved, for all his peculiarities. The desert life, which has filled the Arab with poetry and a sense of the higher mysteries, has sapped the last remnant of idealism from the Trek-Boer's nature, and left him without an aspiration or a dream. The usual lack of fresh meat and the absence of green vegetables as an item in his diet, has reacted upon his physique and made him listless and slouching in gait and deportment, as well as anaemic and prone to disease. This is especially true of his womankind, who, besides being extremely short-lived have, as a rule, lost nearly all pretensions to beauty of face or form.

Bushmanland might be described as a desert, the aridity of which is tempered by occasional thunderstorms. Its bounds begin immediately to the eastward of the rugged mountain chain which runs parallel with the coast-line, about eighty miles inland, and it stretches on for hundreds of miles until merged with the central Karoo plains. These also form its indefinite boundary to the southward. It is, for the most part, almost absolutely level. To the northward, however, a chain of mountains, occasionally very lofty, arises. For stern, uncompromising aridity, for stark, grotesque, naked horror, these mountains stand probably unsurpassed on the face of the globe. Composed of deep brown granite, with here and there immense veins, or patches many miles in extent, of jet-black, shining ironstone, they absorb the torrid sunshine all day, becoming almost red-hot in the process. At night this heat is radiated rapidly at high sunlight power, until the furnace of midnight becomes like an ice-house at dawn.

The only vegetation to be found among these mountains is a species of deadly Euphorbia—formerly much used by the Bushmen in poisoning their arrows—and a few stunted shrubs which are rooted deep down in the crannies, and which put forth a little timid foliage in the cooler season. The only animals are "klipspringers"—antelopes very like the chamois in form and habit; leopards which prey upon these; badgers, wild cats, jackals of several kinds, an occasional hyaena, desert mice, snakes, gorgeously hued lizards and fierce tarantulas. A few large brown hawks hover above the gloomy gorges and wake weird and depressing echoes with their shrill screams.

To the north of this almost impenetrable region the great "Gariep"—the "Yellow River" of the Hottentots—now called the "Orange" in honour of a former Stadtholder of the Netherlands, has carved out a gorge for its devious course, thousands of feet in depth. Allowing for its many and abrupt windings, this gorge, from the point at which the river hurtles into it over an obstinate stratum of rock at what is known as the Augrabies Falls, must be over four hundred miles in length. The greater part of this gorge is unexplored, being totally inaccessible.

Like the Nile, the Orange River drains an immense area of fertile country which is subject to heavy summer rains. It flows down in a raging, brimming flood, which is charged with rich alluvium, during several months of the year. Unlike the Nile, it has carved for itself a deep and narrow channel, through which it hurls its fertilising load with resistless momentum into the ocean which needs it not. Under different circumstances its valley might have been the cradle of another civilisation, and another Sphinx, of Hottentot or Bantu physiognomy, might have stood, gazing through forgotten centuries, across the waste of Bushmanland.

No more dreary prospect can be imagined than that afforded by Bushmanland in its normal condition of drought. After rain, however, it turns for a few short weeks into a smiling garden. This is especially the case around the northern and western margins where, among the rocky kopjes forming the fringe of the plain, gorgeous flowers cover the ground with vivid patches of colour, and climb and trail over the grey stones. This combination always suggests to the traveller a skull crowned with flowers. The stark rocks, blasted by aeons of burning sunshine, are always in evidence, and the wanton luxuriance of the garlands seem to mock at and accentuate their death-like rigour.

The grass with which the greater part of the plain is covered grows in thick shocks some thirty inches in height, from raised tussocks about six feet apart. In dry weather the fibre of the grass crumbles away in dust and the tussock turns black. After rain, however, the new blades shoot out with marvellous rapidity, and the Desert becomes a sea of waving plumes, which are tinted a beautifully delicate green. Between the tussocks spring up flowers of marvellous colour, scent, and form. It has been libellously affirmed that the flowers of the Desert have no scent. It is true that in the hot, midday glare all are more or less scentless, but in the early morning or when the afternoon cools the heliophilas, the pelargoniums, the many species of lily, and others too numerous to particularise, often make the Desert a veritable "scented garden."

The great plain is almost absolutely treeless. Only in one or two localities are a few acacias found. These are of very large size. They are called "Camel-thorns," for the reason that the camelopard was fond of browsing upon their foliage. Amongst the branches are often found the enormous nests of the sociable grosbeaks, sometimes ten feet in diameter. These nests are veritable cities—inhabited by countless numbers of birds. Woe betide the exhausted hunter who seeks the deceitful shade of these trees, for the ground beneath is full of the dreaded "sampans," which bury themselves in the flesh and cause serious injury.

In the fringe of kopjes grow immense aloes (*Aloe dichotoma*—probably closely allied botanically to the almost extinct "Dragon Tree" of Teneriffe). These sometimes reach a height of sixty feet, and may measure twenty feet around their ridged and gnarled trunks. This tree is locally known as the "koekerboom," or "quiver-tree," a reminiscence of the fact that the Bushmen used to remove the fibrous wood from a section of a bough and utilise the cylinder of tough bark as a quiver for their poisoned arrows. The koekerbooms are believed to be of immense age; the oldest Trek-Boers will point to small trees growing close to their favourite camping-places, and tell you that they have not sensibly increased in size in upwards of half a century. Their appearance is extremely belated and archaic.

Running through Bushmanland from north-east to south-west is a curved ridge which is known as the "Jacht Bult," or "hunt-ridge," from the plentifulness of game upon it. This ridge rises so gradually from each side that its very existence is not apparent except for a few minutes at morning and evening—and then only if one happens to be on the top of it. Here occurs a curious phenomenon; for, just as the sun is touching the western horizon, if one looks eastward he will be startled at seeing half of the immense plain shrouded in almost complete darkness. The illusion is due to the western plain being flooded with sunlight whilst from the other the sunlight is suddenly and completely cut off. When the sun sinks the illusion vanishes and the eastern plain appears to be no darker than the western. At sunrise these conditions are, of course, reversed.

This region is the home of the "springbuck," which still survives in countless myriads. After a large "trek," as the annual migration of these animals across the Desert is called, has taken place, the wake of the host looks like an irregularly-ploughed field. Every vestige of vegetation is beaten out by the small, sharp, strong hoofs. It seems at such times as if all the springbucks in the Desert were suddenly smitten by a mad desire to collect and dash towards a certain point.

The springbucks as a rule live without drinking. Sometimes, however—perhaps once in ten years—they develop a raging thirst, and rush madly forward until they find water. It is not many years ago since millions of them crossed the mountain range and made for the sea. They dashed into the waves, drank the salt water, and died. Their bodies lay in one continuous pile along the shore for over thirty miles, and the stench drove the Trek-Boers who were camped near the coast far inland.

The oryx, or, as it is called in South Africa, the "gemsbok," is still to be found in considerable numbers in the vicinity of the great and almost inaccessible sand-dunes which encroach into the desert at several points along its northwestern margin. The gemsbok manages to live without drinking water, finding a substitute in a large, succulent root which grows in the driest parts of the dunes, and which the animal digs up from deep in the sand with its hoofs. A few hartebeests are also to be found. Immense wild bustards, or, as they are called, "paauws," come over from the Kalihari Desert in large flocks. From the same place the desert grouse, which strongly resembles the sand-grouse of Central Asia, throng over in countless myriads. These collect around the open water-places every morning when the sun begins to sting. One dip of water they must have. If the sportsman is hard-hearted enough to remain close to the water-hole, they circle round and round uttering their plaintive cry in a myriad-voiced chorus of strange twitterings. Should the day be hot and no other water obtainable in the neighbourhood—as is often the case—they will drink at one's very feet. From their cry the colloquial name of "kalkivain" is derived.

In hot weather one may trace the zigzag spoor of many a yellow cobra across the sands. By day these creatures remain underground among the mouse-burrows—for they could not live upon the scorching sand—but at night they wander far and near. The horned adder—identical in species with the "worm of old Nile" with which Cleopatra eased herself of her burthen of life—abounds at the roots of the small shrubs and grass-tussocks, where it burrows into the sand to escape the heat, or when hibernating.

Above all, however, Bushmanland is the home of the wild ostrich. Here, in spite of the number of their enemies, human or other, these noble birds are still to be found in considerable numbers. Their booming note heard at night across the waste strongly suggests the distant roar of a hungry lion. When one thinks of the number and ingenuity of the ostrich's enemies one wonders that any still exist. Around every nest that one finds are sure to be several jackals and white crows. The jackal rolls the eggs about by butting them with his nose, and thus dashes, them against each other until they break; the white crow carries stones up into the air and drops them from a height among the eggs, smashing them and befouling the nest with what it is unable to gorge of the contents of the shell; the prowling Hottentot, or half-breed, will follow for days on the spoor until he finds the nest and rifles it.

This region was once the favourite haunt of the Bushman, and long after that unhappy race had disappeared from other parts it here maintained itself. At every water-place may still be seen the polished grooves in the rocks wherein they sharpened their arrows and bone skinning-knives; fragments of their rude pottery lie thickly strewn around. Mixed with the latter may be found, sometimes in considerable quantities, the broken weapons of stone which belonged to a still older race, and which, perhaps, was driven from the face of the land by the Bushmen, as we have driven the latter, and as we ourselves may be driven by some race developing a "fitness" superior to our own.

These water-places would thus seem to be of immense antiquity, and the inference suggests that the climatic conditions of this end of the African continent have not changed appreciably for ages.

The names of a few of these places in the Bushman tongue still survive. Some are very suggestive, and indicate that the Bushman was not totally devoid of sentiment. The following are specimens of local Bushman topography: "Place of Bleeding," "Withered Flower," "Eggshell Cheeks," "Reed-Possessor," "Take-away-from-me-what-I-have-gained," "Place-where-you-may-dig-out-a-little-pot-of-water."

The Bushman used poisoned arrows. He obtained the poison usually from three distinct sources, namely, the poison gland of the puffadder, the black tarantula, and the deadly euphorbia which grows in the river gorge. These he mixed in a paste and smeared upon the sides of his arrow blade. This poison is extremely deadly in its effects, but it works far more rapidly in the system of a ruminating animal than in that of a man. The Bushman could also, however, run game down by sheer fleetness of foot—running until blown and then handing the chase over to another hunter who had posted himself upon the course which, by instinct, he had known the animal would most likely take.

The ostrich was the Bushman's favourite and most profitable quarry. Dressed in the plumes of a former victim he would stalk into the midst of a troop and lay its members low one by one. When he found a nest he would pierce the ends of each egg and blow out the contents. Then, after carefully washing out the shell, he would fill it with water and close up each aperture with a wooden peg. The shell would be buried deep in the sand against contingencies of drought. By some secret sign the members of each clan would know the exact spots where water had thus been buried by their friends, and thus often avoid death by thirst when travelling or hunting.

The Bushman was the true Ishmaelite; he was bound to be eliminated. As a matter of fact there is no room for a Bushman and any one else in any given area, no matter how large.

In the region described the Bushmen have left no record in the shape of paintings on the rocks, which are so common in other parts. This may perhaps be accounted for by the porous nature of many of the low krantzes in which the caves they occupied are situated. It may be, however, that the plants from which their pigments were obtained do not grow in this arid region.

When rain has fallen freely, as it occasionally does, the Trek-Boers flock into Bushmanland from its fringe, upon which they are always hanging. A few weeks of dry weather, however, suffices to dry up the moisture from the shallow, sand-clogged basins, and the country once more becomes a solitude.

For some natures this region possesses a deep and abiding charm. The fresh, crisp air of early morning; the peace which sinks like a benediction upon the wearied earth when the scorching sun has fallen from the sky, and the sand gives off its heat in rapid radiation; the sense of immensity made manifest in the wide, wide plains by day, and in the almost supernaturally bright skies at night; the booming of the ostriches, the bellowing of the rutting springbucks; the queer, snarling yelp of the jackals and the "tshok-tshok" of the paauw as it shakes out its plumes to the rising sun—and who can define the vivid delight which these have brought? Who that has ever been fortunate enough to experience it can recall without a quickening pulse the mad gallop for miles across the plains after a herd of gemsbok, or the fierce rapture of meeting the noble brute at bay, and slaying the only animal of the antelope tribe that has heart enough to face a lion?

It is among the dwellers of this region that the scene of the following tale is laid. These people have but few ideas, and a vocabulary of little more than three hundred words to express these ideas in. The Bible is the only book they ever read, and of that they do not understand more than half the sense. In all essentials, however, they are of the same mould as other men. They live and love, hate and die, in very much the same manner as do other human creatures. It is in the incidentals that the reader may find some difference between these people and the dwellers in more fortunate climes.

Chapter Two.

The Patriarch of Namies.

There was only one camp at Namies (pronounced "Namees"), for all the wells but one had run dry. It was somewhat early in summer, and as yet no thunderstorms had visited the immediate neighbourhood. The camp consisted of a wagon with a fore-and-aft canvas hood, or, as it is called in South Africa, a "tent." On either side of it stood, respectively, a mat-house and a square tent. The particular Trek-Boer who was the owner of this establishment was a somewhat distinguished specimen of his class. Old Schalk Hattingh had, like his father before him, lived his life upon the fringes of the Bushmanland Desert. Tall and corpulent, with a long, silvery-white beard, he spent his days sitting in a big, cushionless, wooden chair. This chair would, according to the weather, be placed either just inside or just outside the mat-house. His legs had become too weak to sustain his large body, so he was only able to walk with the assistance of a long, strong Stick, which never was out of the reach of his hand. In the coldest weather he wore no warmer clothing than a shirt of unbleached calico—always open at the throat, and thus revealing a large area of red skin—a cheap and very thin corduroy coat, a pair of breeches, much too short for him, of tanned sheepskin, and a jackal-skin cap. These clothes he invariably slept in; in fact, the tradition as to when he had last taken them off had been long since lost. On his extremely large feet he wore "veldschoens" of his own make. Socks he would have looked upon as a criminal luxury; pocket-handkerchiefs he had never used in the whole course of his life. Winter and summer he sat, drinking weak coffee all day long, smoking strong tobacco at intervals, and continually expectorating in all directions.

Namies was his headquarters, and had been so for nearly forty years. His well was the best there. Even that, however, ran dry during the early part of summer about once in three years, and he would then shift his camp to some more fortunate spot. But he was always the last to leave and the first to return. No one ever dreamt of camping upon Old Schalk's favourite spot or taking possession of his well, yet to these he had no special right which could be legally enforced.

Old Schalk was a well-known character, and was looked upon as a patriarch and an oracle by the Trek-Boers for hundreds of miles around. He had been a famous man in his day, and could tell interesting, semi-veracious anecdotes of adventures with Bushmen, lions, and other things—predatory or preyed upon. He had never seen a village in his life, excepting the adventitious assemblages of the Trek-Boers. He was known to be a hard man at a bargain, and extremely avaricious; nevertheless he was poor. A few years previous to the period at which this tale opens he had been rich in flocks and herds. Then came the inevitably recurring drought, this time one of exceptional severity. The sheep and goats became thinner and thinner, until they were too weak to go abroad and seek for pasturage. They lay on the sand all day long, eyeing piteously the troughs to which their diminishing dole of water was lifted from the well by the creaking derrick. At last the maddened cattle flung themselves down the well, and their ruined owners were hardly able to drag themselves to the arid banks of the Orange River down the sand-choked gorge at Pella. Here was at least water to drink.

Old Schalk, like most of his neighbours, found himself a poor man. Since the famine he had managed to get a little stock together again, but he was in debt to several Jew hawkers, and had some difficulty in keeping his head above water.

He held the appointment under Government of Assistant Field Cornet. It was his duty in this capacity to report all crimes to the Special Magistrate, to arrest criminals, and to hold inquests in cases of deaths by violence in regard to which there was no suspicion of foul play. This office gave him a certain position among the Trek-Boers and added considerably to his influence.

Old Schalk's wife was only a few years younger than himself, but, as is especially the case with Boer women, she looked much older. His special grievance against Providence was that Mrs Hattingh had lived so long, and thus kept him out of the enjoyment of the charms of younger women.

"There is my brother Gert," he would say in moments of confidence, and without considering whether his wife were present or not, "he has now married his third wife; Willem only the other day lost his second; Jan, who is fifteen years younger than I, buried his first wife only five months ago and is going to marry a fine young girl at the next Nachtmaal—and here I am still sitting with my old 'Bogh',"—a word which may be freely translated as "frump."

From Old Schalk's point of view he undoubtedly had a grievance, for one rarely meets an old Boer—and more especially a Trek-Boer—who has not been married several times.

Mrs Hattingh never appeared to be hurt by such outbursts against unpropitious Fate. She had no intention of dying just yet; sentiment was to her unknown, and she had always taken life philosophically.

"Ja," she would sometimes rejoin, "it is true that I am an old 'Bogh,' but there's not a woman in Bushmanland who can sew karosses as well as I; and if it had not been for the money you got from the Jews for those I made from the skins of the sheep that died in the drought, you would not have any stock to-day."

"Ja; that is true," Old Schalk would grudgingly admit.

"And you would be a fine one to follow a young wife about and keep her in order; with those legs you could not walk the length of the trek-chain."

Old Schalk always resented any reference to his unserviceable legs, so his wife usually had the last word at these discussions.

The junior members of the Hattingh family consisted of two granddaughters and a grand-niece. The sons and daughters of the camp had married and were scattered over the fringe of the Desert. The three girls were orphans. The two granddaughters were tall, listless-looking girls, with dark hair and eyes, and that transparent and unhealthy complexion which sometimes gives a fugacious beauty and is often found in young women whose diet does not embrace a sufficiency of green vegetable food. Their chests were hollow, their shoulders drooped, and they looked incapable of taking much interest in anything. Their ages were respectively, eighteen and nineteen; their names—Maria and Petronella.

Their cousin, Susannah, was a girl of a different type. She was small of stature, well built, and had a keen and alert look. Her features were strongly marked, her eyes and hair were black, and the redness of her lips was rendered more striking by the pallor of the rest of her face. Her movements were distinguished by an energy which was in striking contrast to the listlessness of the other girls. She suggested a well-favoured squirrel among a family of moles. Her features had a strongly Jewish cast. Although not much admired by the young Boers with whom she came in contact—probably because she did not reach their standard of stoutness—she would have been in other surroundings considered a very pretty girl. There was some mystery in connection with her parentage which gave rise to whisperings among the women. It was, however, certain that she was the daughter of one of Old Schalk's nieces.

The spot known as Namies is marked by a few stony, irregular kopjes which lie like a small archipelago in the ocean-like waste of the Bushmanland Desert, not far from its northern margin. The highest of these kopjes is less than four hundred feet above the general level of the plains; a circle two miles in circumference would enclose them all. They are formed of piles of granite boulders, between which grow a few hardy shrubs and koekerbooms.

Chapter Three.

Max.

Max Steinmetz stood in the doorway of the little iron shanty at Namies, which was built near the foot of a kopje about three hundred yards from the Hattingh camp. Above his head was a signboard bearing the legend: "Nathan Steinmetz, Allegemene Handelaar." (General dealer.) He looked out over the wide, wide Desert and watched the smoke-like courses of the violent gusts against which a thunderstorm was labouring from the north-east. The unsavoury odour of half-dried hides assailed his nostrils; the ramshackle iron roof rattled to the blasts over his head. The season was February, and the tortured plains glowed with absorbed heat like Milton's burning marl.

Over the intermittent moaning and howling of the wind could be heard, at intervals, the mutterings of thunder. The Desert now became a roaring blast-furnace, fanned by the sand-laden gusts which raged fiercer and ever fiercer. Max closed the door and barred it from the inside. A few gouts of rain began to thud on the roof. Then a jagged shaft of lightning shot from the zenith, shattered itself into coruscating splinters against some tempest-packed sheaf of air, and seemed to fill the universe with a blinding blaze. At the same instant the winds were stunned by a crash so awful that the solid earth reeled from the shock. Then came the rain in dense, white, lashing waves, and in a few moments the wide plain became a hissing sea.

The storm-cloud rolled away as quickly as it had come, leaving only a few torn wisps of fleecy cloud to mark its wake. Through these the purified sky seemed to open in vaults of azure that pierced the infinite. For a short time the sun flooded the plain with gold and rubies; then it sank, and the cool, quickening evening died in peaceful splendour in the transfigured west.

The storm over, Max opened the door and stepped outside. His first glance was towards the Hattingh camp. Then he brought a chair and a book out of the shop and sat down where, pretending to read, he could look over the top of the page in the same direction. Soon afterwards Susannah came out of the mat-house and superintended the lighting of a fire by the Hottentot maid in the kitchen-scherm, the bushes of which, scattered by the storm, had been rearranged. She had discarded her cappie, and her luxuriant black hair was blown about by the moist breeze. She gave one hurried glance towards the shop and then stood with her back towards it. Max saw this and, in his inexperience, felt saddened.

Max had a face which, had Raphael seen it through the bars of the Ghetto gate at Rome, would have made him take pains to secure the young Jew as a model. It was one of those faces which one only—and that but very rarely—sees in the youth of Israel. Its shape was a pure oval. The skin was a clear olive, and the eyes were large, dark, and melting. His jet-black hair clustered over a broad, low forehead, and his full, red lips were arched like the bow of the Sun-God. As yet the stress of trade had not awakened the ancestral greed which would one day dominate his blood and modify his physiognomy. Small in stature and of perfect symmetry, he did not give one the idea of possessing either strength or activity; in feet he looked like a languorous human exotic who had strayed from the canvas of some "Old Master" whose brush was dedicated to physical beauty. His age was twenty-one, but he looked several years younger.

Max was a clerk at a very small salary in the employ of his brother Nathan. The business was a paying one, but the carrying of it on involved extremely hard work. Nathan spent most of his time in moving about from camp to camp among the Trek-Boers and the half-breeds who dwelt among the saltpans in the central and southern portions of the Desert. He travelled with a small, strong cart, which was drawn by six hardy but debilitated-looking donkeys. His practice was to leave Namies with a load of hucksters' merchandise and to return, generally about two months afterwards, with a quantity of ostrich feathers. The Desert abounded in wild ostriches which, although protected by law, were ruthlessly hunted down for the sake of their feathers. There was, of course, a certain risk of discovery involved, and this would have been followed by heavy penalties, but

Nathan was prepared to take this risk for the sake of the large profits which he made. The feathers of the wild ostrich fetch a much higher price than those of the domesticated bird. In many of the waste places of South Africa the protecting law is often but a name. Nathan knew that the risk of his being convicted was very small. Just now he was absent upon a trip, but his return was daily expected. In the meantime Max had charge of the store.

Nathan and Max were orphans, and had been brought up by an uncle —a pawnbroker of the East End of London. Their parents were German Jews who had settled in England. They had no brothers or sisters. Eight years previously the uncle had given Nathan a hundred pounds and sent him to the Cape to seek his fortune. Four years afterwards Max followed. In the meantime Nathan had made a little money as a "smouse," or hawker. With Max's assistance he was able to extend his operations considerably. For the first two years the younger brother had worked without any salary; then, at the instance of the uncle, who made particular inquiries upon the point, Max was given a small stipend.

Chapter Four.

Spring's Idyll.

The next day was a dream of delight. The evaporation from the sand counteracted the heat of the sun, and the pungent air was full of germinating energy. Cool, gentle breezes awoke now and then, wandered vaguely to and fro, and then laid themselves down to rest, rising anon to play in a circle of mimic whirlwinds. Old Schalk sat in the doorway of the mat-house with his feet in the sun and the large Bible open upon his knees. The combination of Old Schalk and an open Bible meant either that he was in extremely good humour and felt at peace with all mankind and in general harmony with his environment—or else the direct reverse. In the former case he would usually have the volume open at the Song of Solomon; in the latter, at the 109th Psalm. To-day he prayed, although he knew it not, for his heart was lifted up in involuntary thankfulness and appreciation of the feast which was so lavishly spread around him. His happiness was even beyond the terms of his favourite Psalms, which he knew off by heart—even the numbers of the great lyric poets of Israel seemed to fall short of the music which Nature was making upon his worn heart-strings.

Mrs Hattingh was sitting boiling soap inside the kitchen-scherm, her failing eyes rendered more than usually red and rheumy by the steam arising from the acrid lye. She, too, felt the benign influences with which the Desert was rich; the labour she was engaged in was not as irksome as usual. As she broke the bushes into the soap-pot she might have been a rapt sorceress brewing a love-philtre, or a priestess sacrificing at the shrine of the God of Cleanliness.

Maria and Petronella were sitting on the wagon-box crooning a weird song in a minor key. They felt sleepy and happy, for Mother Nature had a word for them too. It was a word very softly spoken, and in a language which they did not yet fully understand, but it made them dream vague, sweet dreams. Susannah heard the voice, and, low as it was spoken, it awoke her and she hearkened to it. She, too, failed to understand the words, but the cadences were sweet and seemed to be full of an infinite promise.

Nature, in her spring guise, has to do her work in the Desert, when she does it at all, in a hurry. There the seasons do not follow the regular course. At the end of her summer revel in other southern lands she sometimes suddenly bethinks her that away to the northward she has been for long neglectful of her duties, so she flies to the arid plains, where perhaps the very traces of her footprints have been long since forgotten. Then with a sudden dower of riches she tries to make amends for her forgetfulness; she tarries for a few sweet, pregnant hours, and the ardours and burgeonings of a season are consummated in one delicious day.

Susannah felt the rapid sap of sudden springtime rise in a sweet storm to her heart and to her brain. It seemed to her as though she had wings, and she longed to fly out over the infinite waste and beyond the blue, mysterious haze in which it merged with the horizon in a sapphire ring. The highest of the little group of kopjes stood just at the back of the camp, and her senses bounded at the thought of climbing quickly to the summit and thus getting so much nearer the sky. A tall koekerboom which stood on the very top quivered in the wind, and every cluster of leaves at the ends of its dichotomous branches seemed to beckon to her to come.

She climbed into the wagon, opened the camphor-wood box in which she kept her limited wardrobe, and selected her best dress. This was a cheap print, delicately flowered, and of soft hues. It thus afforded a pleasing contrast to the gaudy and crudely coloured habiliments of her cousins. After she had put it on one might have seen that the dress fitted her neat figure like a new glove. Her ample hair she rolled into a knot, but, after a moment's consideration, she uncoiled it again and shook it back over her shoulders. Then she put on a "cappie" made of print of the same pattern as her frock. A cheap necklet of coral completed her toilet. She clasped this hurriedly about her throat as she sprang to the ground from the back of the wagon. She panted with desire to get away to the high peak where the solitary koekerboom, which had defied the sun for centuries, stood beckoning to her, and any delay was a pain. She sped away among the aromatic shrubs that clustered among the impassive granite rocks on the side of the kopje, and the brown stones she trod on seemed to be as buoyant as the air that filled her veins with ecstasy. In a few minutes she had gained the top of the kopje, when she sank down in pleasant exhaustion at the foot of the hoar-ancient koekerboom.

As she ascended the kopje the breeze freshened, and the stiff, awkward branches of the archaic tree seemed to be seized with excitement unfitting its age and experience; it beckoned violently, and until Max, who was standing at the door of the shop, saw not alone its signal, but the flutter of the delicately flowered print dress which at that moment was rippling against its gnarled knees.

Max hurriedly locked the shop and sped up the side of the kopje towards the antiquated tree, which now seemed to have fallen asleep, so still it was. Schalk Hattingh's was the only camp then at Namies, and as Nathan had given strict injunctions that the Hattinghs were to have no more credit, nothing was to be lost in respect of their custom. Max would, he told himself, be able to descry any approaching customers from the top of the kopje.

Susannah heard the nearing footstep. She had now taken off her cappie, and was lying back between two of the shapeless roots which were continuations of flanking buttresses thrown out by the tree towards the north-east, from whence the storms had been trying to uproot it—probably ever since the days when the galleys of Pharaoh passed down the Red Sea and returned to Egypt through the Pillars of Hercules. The girl arose into a sitting posture and turned towards the boy a face flushed with exercise and eyes liquid with delight. Max put out his hand in mute greeting, and she clasped it silently. Then he threw himself on the ground at her feet.

These two had for some time attracted each other. On Max's side the attraction had lately begun to ripen into something very like love. But of this as yet he was unaware. To-day the universe seemed to breathe of music, the boughs of the old tree and the granite rocks were as the strings of a sounding harp, touched by the wind as a plectrum.

Spring, in a graciously capricious moment, resolved to crown her holiday with an idyll. Max arose and held out his hand to the girl. She took it, and he drew her gently to her feet. They wandered on together with scanty, broken speech and averted eyes, through lately arid nooks and hollows made sweet and full of the promise of verdure by yesterday's rain. The faint-green spear-points of strange vegetation were already piercing the brown earth; quaint beetles crawled out from under the stones and beat their soft "tok-tok-tok" on the ground, signalling to prospective mates; lizards of a deeper and more vivid blue than anything else in Nature's storehouse, sunned themselves on the rocks, panting with enjoyment.

They came to a flowering mass of gethyllis—that strange plant the curled leaves of which wind out their spirals in winter to catch the dewdrops and conduct them down their tube-like channels to the deep-underground bulb, which waits until the fiercest sun of summer shines before it sends up its lovely, tulip-like cup of snowy white or vivid crimson. The luscious scent filled the air and caused a faint, delicious intoxication. They bent over the blossoms and began gathering them. In doing this their hands met by accident and they started apart suddenly, thrilling with unknown confusion.

Their faltering speech died away altogether, and they more than ever avoided each other's gaze. After retracing their steps for a short distance they again paused. The vague horizon seemed to become of absorbing interest. Each felt to blame for the abashment of the other, and both seemed to drink of a cup of humiliation. The old tree waved sympathetically over them its topmost branches, in which the wind seemed to waken a sigh.

Careless Nature, to bring them together, sacrificed a life. She sent a message down through a cleft in the rock against which Susannah was dejectedly leaning, and called from the depths where it had long been sleeping a poisonous red centipede. The creature crawled down over the girl's shoulder and endeavoured to enter her sleeve at the wrist. Then Max saw it. He sprang forward in a spasm of terror, brushed the centipede aside with his hand; not, however, before it had given him a venomous nip. In an instant he had crushed the life out of the creature with his foot; then, with an exclamation of pain, he turned towards the girl. His hand was already beginning to swell. Susannah tore a piece off the curtain of her cappie and began to bind up the injury. As she did so she came so close that she leant slightly against Max. Then the opportunity triumphed over the pain—he passed his arm around her, drew her to him, and kissed her on the quivering lips.

The centipede and its sting were soon forgotten. Nature held them, embraced and embracing, for a blissful eternity; they saw the face of happiness smiling in the rosy gloom under Love's wing.

The koekerboom became wrapped in a whirlwind of excitement, its gaunt boughs swayed until they clashed, and the sap rose in its slowly beating heart until the yellow buds which a few of its less mature twigs had put forth tentatively, as though half ashamed of such frivolity, burst open and sent forth a faint shower of pollen, which fell like a spangling of gold-dust upon Susannah's hair.

As they paced away, hand in hand, a small army of fierce desert ants were dragging away the still writhing body of the centipede to their underground storehouse. Nature, so very lavish in large matters, is extremely economical in trifles.

Chapter Five.

Gert Gemsbok.

Gert Gemsbok prowled along the bank of the Orange River and bent an attentive eye upon the brimming flood. The great stream, swollen by the summer rains in far-off Basutoland, sped roaring down the rapids just above the Augrabies Falls, over which it would plunge into that mysterious, unexplored gorge through which its secret way lay for some four hundred miles to the Atlantic Ocean. Brown with the gleanings of tens of thousands of square miles of loamy hill and dale swept by furious thunderstorms, clogged with the detritus gathered from flooded flat and spate-ravaged kloof, foul with the rubbish from many a distant mining camp on the banks of its tributary, the Vaal, the torrent swept irresistibly on with a growling roar, the might of which could not be realised without receding for some distance from the bank. Then it would be felt that the air was filled with continuous thunder and that the very earth shuddered with the throbbings of this mighty artery, as the body of a man quivers after unwonted effort.

Flotsam and jetsam abounded in every cranny of the bank and on the down-stream side of every point and headland. Strange objects might be here and there seen—broken packing-cases, dead cattle, sheep, and goats, pumpkins, skins, and old rags. In every bay of still water lay an unsavoury jumble. Gert examined the swollen carcases one by one in the almost vain hope of finding one not too decomposed to eat.

Walking upstream he crossed a promontory covered with scrub. Behind this lay an inlet in the bank which was filled by a slow swirl generated by a rapid immediately above. He paused and cast his eye over the different objects which were slowly circling round and round. One of these soon riveted his attention: it was a rough wooden framework superimposed upon a strong raft, on which was stretched the body of a man dressed in European clothing. Gert walked round the bend of the inlet until he reached a convenient spot on its opposite face. His practised eye recognised this as the place where the object of his scrutiny would most probably ground or come close enough to the bank to be caught hold of, if necessary. Having reached the spot in question, he sat down on a willow stump and waited. The wooden raft with its gruesome burden kept for some time circling slowly round and round the pool, but Gert noticed that at each revolution it seemed to sweep in a little nearer the bank. He began to note the details. The body was that of a very tall man with a full, red beard. He was dressed in a grey flannel shirt, which being slightly open at the throat, revealed a brawny chest covered with russet hair. The nether limbs were clad in moleskin trousers and strong, thick-soled boots such as miners often wear. The feet and arms were securely bound to the sides of the framework.

At length the raft caught against a submerged stump. To this it hung for a moment; then it heeled over and swayed itself loose, and the current washed it slowly against the bank, where it grounded at the watcher's feet.

The body was horrible to look upon; the eyes were sunken out of sight or had decomposed away—the flesh was livid. The wrists were cut by the cords that bound them, showing that the man had been bound living upon the raft. Into the flesh of his forehead the letter "V," about an inch in length, had been cut. Gert waded into the water up to his waist and paused close to the horrible object. His feet were sore from constant wanderings over the stony mountains, and he coveted the dead man's boots. Conquering his repugnance, he drew his knife and severed the laces. Then he pulled the boots off and flung them high on the bank behind him. After pausing for a few seconds he searched the trouser pockets, but found that they contained nothing. As he did this he averted his eyes from the dead face. His search over, he waded along the shore towards the outside limit of the inlet, where the current was strong, drawing the raft after him. Launched forward with his full strength, the raft was caught by the current and swirled out into the mid-stream, where it passed from view into the confused mass of wave-tossed rubbish.

Gert then climbed up the bank and returned to where he had flung the boots. Upon examining these he found that the layers of leather forming the sole of one were gaping widely at the side. He tried to press the layers together, but found that he could not do so owing to the presence of some object which had evidently been inserted between them. He pulled this out and found it to be a piece of rag in which was wrapped a diamond as large as a hazel-nut. Searching farther, he found that in each boot holes had been scooped out in the thick mass of leather above the outer layer, and diamonds inserted. He found six altogether—three in each boot. The stones were pure white, and of that peculiar crystallisation which characterises the gems found on the banks of the Vaal River, as distinguished from those found in what are known as the "dry diggings."

Gert looked at the shining gems as they lay upon his hand and marvelled exceedingly. He knew right well that the stones were diamonds, for he had worked for a year in the Kimberley mine. He also knew that the law forbade him to have such things in his possession, and that if caught with them he would be liable to severe punishment. Yet here, he thought, was the means of attaining riches; surely there must be some way of turning to account the prize which he had honestly obtained? With a spasm of exultant dread he slipped the stones into his skin wallet. Then he placed a heavy pebble into each of the boots and flung them as far as he could into the stream. He sat in thought for a few moments; then he retraced his steps, down-stream, to a spot where had been deposited the only half-decomposed carcase of a goat which he had raked out of the flood. This he shouldered and carried up the rocky gorge in which the cave was situated, in which he dwelt with his mother and his wife.

By this time the wooden raft with its dread enigma had been whirled down the rapids and dashed to pieces over the Augrabies Falls. What dread tragedy had resulted in the voyage of this ark with its single gruesome passenger upon the bosom of the brown flood through the scorched Desert—what terrible act of crime or retribution had sent this sign to be revealed for an instant to the startled ken of a prowling savage, will probably never be explained until all mysteries are unlocked!

Gert Gemsbok, the Koranna Hottentot, was a remarkable man. In the rebellion of the Griqua and Koranna Clans, which broke out upon the northern border of the Cape Colony in 1879, he had taken a prominent part. Captured with arms in his hands and identified as having led a certain band of rebels which was concerned in some serious depredations, he was sentenced by the Special Court to a severe flogging and a long term of imprisonment. He served the first part of his sentence at the Breakwater Convict Station, Cape Town, but was afterwards transferred to one of the Diamond Mining Compounds at Kimberley. Upon his discharge he took service as a labourer at the mines, with the view of making sufficient money to enable him to return half-way across the continent to the Desert which he loved, and somewhere within the indefinite bounds of which he hoped to find traces of his family. He attained his object; he found his old mother and his wife living close to Namies in Bushmanland, in great misery from want, and suffering from incurable disease. His two children were dead. The two women were unwholesome and in every way unpleasant to look upon, besides being almost helpless, but Gert, no less than they, was happy in the reunion.

Having still a few pounds left from his earnings at the diamond fields, he bought a few articles of clothing for the two women from a wandering hawker. Then the problem as to how they were to exist loomed up. Gert could easily get work among the Trek-Boers, as a shepherd, but how was he to support the two helpless women out of his earnings, which only amounted to eight fat-tailed sheep per annum? The thing was almost impossible, but he succeeded in doing it.

Soon, however, he again fell upon evil days. This time he suffered for righteousness' sake. The Hottentots are, probably, the most untruthful race under the sun, but this Hottentot invariably made a point of telling the truth, and misfortune fell upon him in consequence. A certain Trek-Boer named Willem Bester was charged with a serious crime before the Special Magistrate for the Northern Border. Gert, unfortunately for himself, had been a witness to the act, and was, accordingly, called upon to give evidence. Instead of sensibly lying, and thus exonerating the accused, who was related to his master, poor Gert injudiciously told the truth. As a result Bester was convicted and sentenced to a long term of imprisonment. The consequences were disastrous to the veracious exception to the rule of his race. He was dismissed from his employment and turned adrift. He tried to obtain service everywhere, but found that he was boycotted—driven away with contumely from every Trek-Boer's camp at which he applied.

So the three miserable beings wandered about the Desert from water-place to water-place, digging for "veld-kost"—the generic name by which the many species of edible bulbs, leaves, and tubers with which the fringe of the Desert abounds, are known. In the short and adventitious spring, when the leaves appearing through the sand indicated the proper spots to dig at, life was comparatively easy, but after the northern winds had scorched away the herbage it was only by a bitter struggle that body and soul could be kept together. Each year, when the Orange River came down in flood, the three wretched creatures would occupy a cave close to its southern bank just above the Augrabies Falls. Here, especially when the rains had been very heavy in the Orange Free State or the upper reaches of the Vaal River, they used to reap a rich harvest of garbage.

Six years of this life had passed prior to the finding of the mysterious corpse and the diamonds.

The cave was an oval chamber in the sheer granite wall in which the flank of a mighty mountain ended. The floor was of dry sand, and there was no drip from the smoke-stained roof to cause inconvenience. Here it was cool in the hottest weather, and when the cold eastern winds shrieked in arid wrath down the black gorges, the three waifs lay snug and warm. The furniture of the cave consisted of a few miserable skins, two or three earthern pots of native make, a bow and a quiverful of poisoned arrows, and a few blunted iron spikes, the latter being used in the root-digging operations. A musical instrument, which will hereafter be described, completes the inventory.

Gert was an old man. His limbs were half-crippled by rheumatism, and his sight had begun to weaken. The Hottentots are a thin-skinned race, and flogging is to them a very terrible punishment. Gert had never fully recovered from his experience of the lash. Had his physical vigour been greater he might have been able to kill game from time to time, especially when the trek-bucks crossed the Desert. As things were, his hunting never yielded him more than a few snakes and lizards and an occasional jackal. On very rare occasions he managed to get a shot at a klipspringer antelope; only, however, after lying in wait for hours at a time in a red-hot rock-cleft, on the faint chance of the bucks being startled in one of the hollows and running past him on their way to the next. But these waitings were usually unsuccessful and he could not afford to lose the time which they took up.

Gert Gemsbok reached the cave with his unsavoury burthen. This he flung down on the ground outside, for its stench would have made the air of the cave unbearable. It was bad enough to have to eat such stuff without breathing it as well. Having skinned the leg of the carcase he cut up some of the meat and put it into one of the pots. From a crevice in the wall he took out a handful of strong-smelling herbs; these he broke up and added to the stew with the object of deadening the effluvium.

After supper he related his adventure to the two women. The mother was half in her dotage, and had almost reverted to the animal in the course of the years of misery which she had lived through. The wife became wild with excitement at the idea of once more having money and being able to purchase longed-for luxuries. She tried to persuade Gert to start at once on a journey across the Desert to Kenhardt for the purpose of realising his property and obtaining coffee, sugar, and tobacco. The memory of these things, none of which had been tasted for years, continually tantalised her. Gert, however, mindful of former experiences, had no intention of placing himself within the power of the law again.

The old woman had originally come from Great Namaqualand; she belonged to the Bondleswartz Clan. She was continually urging her son to remove to the land of her birth; but this he could never be persuaded to do. He always clung to the hope of being able to remove to some civilised locality where coffee and tobacco would be obtainable.

One mitigation of all this misery existed. This Hottentot was an artist, carrying in his heart a spark of that quality which we call genius, and which might be called the flower that bears the pollen which fertilises the human mind, and without which the soul of man would not exist, nor would his understanding have sought for aught beyond the satisfaction of his material senses. Gert Gemsbok was a musician. His instrument was of a kind which is in more or less common use among the Hottentots, and which is known as a "ramkee." The ramkee is very like a banjo rudely constructed. In the hands of a skilful player its tones may be pleasing to the ear. One peculiarity of the performance is that a great deal of the fingering—if one may use the term—is done with the chin. There are usually four strings, but some instruments contain as many as seven.

In Gert Gemsbok's ramkee the drum was made from a cross section of an ebony log, which had been hollowed out with infinite labour until only a thin cylinder of hard, sonorous wood was left. Across this was stretched the skin of an antelope, and inside were several layers of gum—this for the sake of enriching the tone. The bridge was the breast-bone of a wild goose; the strings were made of the sinews of a number of wild animals, selected after a long series of experiments as to their respective suitability to the different parts of the gamut.

The elder woman was almost totally deaf, and the younger too much preoccupied by her physical ailments to pay much heed to the music. The musician, however, required no audience to enable him to reap the fullest enjoyment from the exercise of his art. He loved music for its proper sake, and under its influence could soar away above his sordid surroundings into a heaven of his own creation.

His favourite air was one which ran somewhat as follows. Upon it he would improvise and invent fantastic arabesques and ingenious variations:—

The old woman became more and more feeble, until at length she seemed to lose every faculty except an appetite for certain kinds of food. She lay for weeks without speaking. One night she surprised the others by complaining, in a very distinct voice, of feeling cold. Gert stirred up the embers and threw a few twigs upon them. Soon after this she said—

"Now I am going over the river."

Next morning they found she was dead.

Gert walled up the mouth of the cave with the heaviest stones he could move, leaving the body inside. Then he and his wife departed. He made up his mind to attempt once more to obtain employment. Perhaps after six years his crime of truth-telling might have been forgotten or condoned. He now had an object in life—the realisation of the property which Fate had thrown in his way. He would first return to Namies, which was a place of congregating for Trek-Boers. Possibly he might be able to get employment there. Even if unsuccessful, however, there was still veld-kost to be had, and there were only two mouths to feed now. Alone, he might easily have made his way to other parts and disposed of the diamonds—even a tithe of their value would have made him a rich man—but his wife could only hobble a couple of miles a day at the very most. He could, of course, have left her to starve, but the thought of doing this never so much as crossed his mind.

So Gert Gemsbok, as stout-hearted as any paladian who ever carried a lance to the Holy Land, packed up his bundle of worn, dirty skins, and tied the pots on the top of it with some withes of twisted bark. He hid his bow and arrows in a dry crevice against the possibility of future needs—they would have been regarded, and rightly so, as the Mark of the Beast among the Trek-Boers. Then, with his ramkee slung under his arm and his miserable old wife hobbling upon cranky legs behind him—blinking in the sunlight to which she had been long unaccustomed—he struck boldly back to renew the battle of life among the men who had driven him forth to herd with the wild beasts.

His six diamonds, wrapped in a dirty rag, were sewn in a row along the bottom of his skin wallet.

Chapter Six.

Too General to be Specified.

When Susannah reached the camp with the afterglow of her lover's kisses still upon her lips, she found that dinner was over. There was a new look upon her face and a light in her eye, which were not lost on any member of the family. She took a rusk from the cupboard and then went to the scherm for a cup of coffee which Katryn, the Hottentot servant-girl, had saved for her. Katryn had seen Max follow Susannah to the kopje, and, as she noticed the new look upon the girl's face, had drawn her own conclusions. After pouring out the coffee she shot an extremely sly glance at Susannah's face and then turned away, her shoulders shaking with laughter.

Old Schalk turned to his wife, who was sitting beside him in the mat-house, hemming an apron—

"Wife, did you see how strange she looked? I wonder what she and the Jew have been doing on the kopje?"

"Let us call her and ask. Susannah!"

"Yes, aunt."

"Where have you been that you did not come to dinner?"

"At the koekerboom on the top of the kopje, aunt."

"Who was with you?"

"Max, aunt."

"What happened to make you look so strange?"

In the most self-possessed manner possible Susannah replied—

"He told me he loved me, and I promised to marry him."

Old Schalk and his wife both gasped; then the old man broke out—

"You promised to marry *him*—a Jew—one of those who denied the Lord Jesus and crucified Him?"

"I am sure Max did not do that; for one thing, he was not born at the time."

"Don't tell me! If he did not do it himself his forefathers did, and the Lord laid a curse on the Jews."

"Who ever heard of such a thing as marrying a Jew?" broke in Mrs Hattingh. "I am sure the minister would refuse you the sacrament if you were to do it."

"I love him, and I will marry no one else," replied Susannah composedly.

"It is not even as if he were rich," continued Mrs Hattingh; "but he has nothing—he is only a servant. The shop belongs to his brother."

Maria and Petronella, were just on the other side of the mat-house wall, listening to all that was said, and giggling and making signs to each other. Old Schalk bethought him of his overdue account at the shop, and wondered how this unexpected development would affect his relations with Nathan, with whom he could not afford to quarrel. But Max was often, as at present, in charge of the business; he also had to be considered. The old Boer came to the conclusion that his safest course was to ignore the whole affair, at all events for the present, until after Nathan's return.

"The idea of her wanting to marry a little boy like that! A nice joke, indeed! When Nathan comes back he will soon put him right."

"And to think of her looking at a fellow of his size when a fine man like Jan Roster, who has plenty of stock and a farm of his own, just wants but a little encouragement to make him have the banns put up for the next Nachtmaal."

Susannah turned away indignantly and left the mat-house. Jan Roster was a young farmer who owned land on the opposite fringe on the Desert, many arid miles from Namies. His business, the peculiar methods of which will be explained later on, sometimes brought him to northern Bushmanland. Recently he had cast looks of tenderness at Susannah. This, however, was not much of a distinction; he was known to be very anxious indeed to get married—in fact, he had proposed to nearly every good-looking girl within two hundred miles of his farm. In spite of his flourishing circumstances, his bulky build, and his not specially ill-favoured appearance, no girl could ever be got to take him seriously. He had spent a few months at a college at Stellenbosch, and thus received what, by courtesy, was termed an education. Theology was his speciality, and could he have conveniently combined the ministry with farming as carried on upon his peculiar lines, he would undoubtedly have attempted to enter the Church. As things were, he was in the habit, when on his rounds, of preaching to the Trek-Boers and half-breeds. It was understood that he was ambitious of entering Parliament eventually, and that he looked upon sermons as a preparation for debating in the senate of his country.

"Is it true that you are going to marry the little Jew?" asked Maria, as Susannah left the mat-house.

Susannah passed on indignantly without deigning an answer. She was not going to stand having her lover referred to in such slighting terms.

It was past eight o'clock when the waning moon looked over the eastern rim of the Desert. Max was sitting on a packing-case outside the shop, trying to make up his mind as to whether he ought to walk over to the camp and see Susannah or not. His heart said "Go," but his reason said "Stay." He instinctively divined that there would be opposition to any connection between himself and Susannah on the part of the Hattinghs. He wondered whether Susannah had told about what had happened. It seemed to him impossible that such a thing could be kept concealed—the clucking lizards which came out of their sand-burrows after the sun had gone down, and the green pneumoras squeaking on the bushes, seemed to be discussing nothing else—to be proclaiming their opinion of the occurrence far and wide. When the moon arose Susannah happened to be watching it as well. Perhaps he saw her face reflected on the gleaming, pearly surface. Max arose from his seat and walked over to the Hattingh camp.

He went straight to Susannah and took her shyly outstretched hand. She returned his ardent pressure slightly, and a spasm of bliss went through him. Then he turned and greeted the others with nervous effusiveness, but his advances were very coolly received. No one volunteered a remark for some little time. The silence became oppressive; it was broken by Old Schalk, in evident pursuance of a conversation which Max's visit had interrupted. He addressed the visitor—

"What is the real belief of the Jews and the Roman Catholics about Christ?"

"I—I don't exactly know," replied Max hesitatingly; "I was very young when I left home."

"But you know well enough," said Mrs Hattingh. "Jan Roster told us all about it in his last sermon: Pontius Pilate and the soldiers were Roman Catholics, and—and—"

"Well, wife, we are waiting."

"Ach, Schalk, you heard the sermon as well as I. At all events the Jews and the Roman Catholics between them crucified the Lord."

"I know that as well as you do, woman; but what I asked about was their belief. Oom Dantje van Rooyen says that he heard from the minister that the Jews and the Roman Catholics do not believe quite the same thing."

"Oh! what should I know about that? But surely" (turning to Max) "you can tell us about your faith?"

Poor Max did not know what to say. Nathan had, over and over again, impressed upon him that, although there was certainly no truth in any religion whatever, he must be sure to keep all the Jewish feasts and observances—with the exception of fasts, which he was to pretend to keep—all the days of his life. He had heard other Jews discussing ritual and religion in the same strain. He wished heartily that he knew the details of Susannah's faith, so that he might believe what she believed. He replied, lamely enough—

"You must ask my brother about these things."

"Another thing I should like to know," said Old Schalk; "that is, why they eat children in the synagogues?"

It was strange to hear this echo of one of the lying cries of the Judenhetze in this remote corner of an African Desert.

"You must wait and ask my brother," repeated Max.

"Yes; they are a wicked lot in their religion," continued Old Schalk. "Fancy a religion that forbids one to eat pork and teaches you to eat children—not their own children, oh no, but Christian children that they steal in the streets of the big towns, and then fatten up for the Passover!"

"But, uncle, I don't think they do so any more," said Susannah, moved by the pain in Max's face. "It was long ago that they used to do that."

"What does a girl like you know about such things? Did we not read about it in the book which Uncle Sarel lent us, and didn't Jan Roster say it was quite true, and that they caught the Jews doing it in Russia the other day? Why, even Max cannot say it isn't true."

"I—I never heard of it," faltered Max.

"Never heard of it?" said Mrs Hattingh in low but indignant tones. "What a dreadful thing to be so ignorant of one's own religion!"

Max went home slightly consoled in his humiliation by another gentle pressure from the hand of Susannah at parting. But some of the bloom had already been rubbed off the blossom which had unfolded in such radiant fairness only a few hours before. He could see that Susannah's secret had been surprised from her, and that opposition and danger loomed ahead. He anticipated that Nathan would make his life a burthen, would torture him with coarse allusions and unpleasant jokes. This he was prepared for, and the prospect was a sickening one. The future was heavily clouded, and behind the clouds visible he foreboded others. But "the thoughts of youth are long, long thoughts." His love was sure, and he knew it to be returned. Sleep knit up the ravelled fabric of his happiness, and memories of the new bliss he had tasted haunted his dreams.

The next morning brought trouble. Shortly after breakfast Max saw, to his dismay, three members of the Hattingh family labouring heavily across the sand towards the shop. Mrs Hattingh was in the centre—she leant heavily on the arms of her granddaughters. As the three entered the shop, the two girls looked at Max with an expression of indescribable slyness. Max groaned in spirit; Nathan had given him strict injunctions that on no account whatever were any members of the Hattingh family to get any more credit. He knew instinctively that this was what they had now come to ask for.

Mrs Hattingh sat down heavily upon a packing-case, panting from the exertions of her walk. Maria and Petronella lifted the flap of the counter quite unceremoniously and walked in. Then they began to pull down the goods from the shelves and examine them. Mrs Hattingh beckoned to Max to come to her. In a low tone and with meaning looks she told him that she wanted to buy some material for a dress for Susannah. Max knew this to be a lie, but he did not dare to show his knowledge. She eventually selected enough material for two dresses; but, from the number of yards ordered, Max could see that his attachment was being used for the purpose of providing the two large specimens of young womanhood present with frocks which they badly needed. Other articles were selected by the girls, who kept darting meaning looks at him and uttering whispered hints about their cousin. When they left, carrying several large parcels, the Hattingh account had been increased on the *debit* side by upwards of two pounds sterling, and the fact pressed like an indigestion upon the already laden breast of poor Max.

Within a few days the Trek-Boers began to flock into Namies. Pasturage was now plentiful, and the gregarious instinct, which is present to a certain extent even in a Trek-Boer, prompted them to draw together. A week after the rain there were fully a dozen camps grouped around that of Old Schalk.

A good deal of flirting of a sort went on among the young men and maidens. Music nightly startled the coneys until they scuttled away among the rocks of the kopje, for "Oom Schulpad" turned up from no one knew where with his old fiddle, and played reels and polkas which made the feet of the young people itch to be dancing.

Oom Schulpad was an elderly and deformed man who owned a disreputable-looking cart and three small donkeys, by means of which he used to make extremely long journeys through the Desert, which he knew as well as he knew his instrument. In many places where another would have died of thirst, Oom Schulpad could find water. Music and hunting were his two passions, and he loved his rifle as much as his fiddle. Sometimes he would penetrate deep into the dunes, and return with a load of gemsbok bultong. He was a thorough vagrant by disposition, and hardly ever settled down at one spot for more than a fortnight at a time. His music made him a *persona grata* at all the camps, so he simply passed from one to another—always a welcome guest.

Being very clever and versatile as a mechanic, he could mend harness, repair a gun, make veldschoens, or replace a broken spoke in the wheel of a wagon. His name, which means "Uncle Tortoise," was given him on account of the shape of his back. He had a real talent as well as a passionate love for music. His tongue was an extremely bitter one, and he was accordingly feared by those whom he disliked. He had never married. He said that he hated women; nevertheless he was usually to be found, when not away hunting, in the company of young girls. These, as a rule, liked and trusted him.

It was with the advent of the Trek-Boers that the real troubles of poor Max began. The relations between himself and Susannah formed the standing joke at Namies for weeks. Every day the shop would be filled with idle young men and women whose only purpose was to joke at the expense of the unhappy lover. Many of these jokes were coarse, and made Max burn with shame. He often longed for muscle so that he might revenge his wrongs. Sometimes the supposed prospective domestic arrangements of the young couple with reference to the extremely limited accommodation at the back of the shop would be discussed in realistic and distressing detail. Attached to the shop was a little room about twelve feet square, which formed a lean-to. This, with the shop and a small room at the back which was used as a store for hides, formed the whole extent of the premises. The back room was occupied by the brothers jointly as a sleeping chamber. Their meals were cooked by a Hottentot boy behind a bush, and were eaten upon the counter.

Susannah also had her troubles, but she did not suffer nearly as much as Max, for she had an extremely bitter tongue, and in the game of chaff was more than a match for any one who attacked her.

These two thus underwent a discipline which stood them in good stead afterwards. In the course of a couple of weeks they became more or less callous, and were it not for the dread of Nathan's return, which oppressed him like a nightmare, Max would have been happy enough. But Nathan was now a fortnight overdue, and was daily expected to arrive.

On the afternoon of the second Sunday after the meeting at the foot of the koekerboom on the top of the kopje, Max suddenly made up his mind and did what was for him a very heroic deed. He put on his best clothes, went boldly over to the Hattingh camp, at which there was a large miscellaneous gathering. He walked around the circle and shook hands with every one present. Then he took his seat next to Susannah, who blushed with pleasure at her lover's daring. She had been rather hurt at the way in which he had kept aloof from her, and his vulnerability to the banter which she despised had annoyed her.

After a few minutes the company was electrified mildly by seeing these two walk off together. This time they did not make for the kopje, but strolled across the flats, where a few springbucks were playing about unconcernedly as though they knew it was Sunday.

Old Schalk snorted violently, and began to mutter questions at his wife. She—her conscience gripping her over the credit which, by virtue of her tacit approval of his addresses towards her niece she had induced Max to give—whispered audibly—

"Ach! what does it matter? Let the children alone."

The conversation soon glided back to the channel in which it had been flowing when the interruption came. A certain stranger—a man who was travelling through Bushmanland for the purpose of buying cattle for the Cape Town market—was discussing astronomy with Old Schalk, who was a strong supporter of the geocentric theory. The cattle-dealer was not by any means well up in his subject; as a matter of fact, he was simply retailing certain notions which he had picked up in a crude state from a young relative of his who had been to a college, and which he had not been able properly to digest. Nevertheless he stoutly maintained his thesis.

"Ach! what?" said Old Schalk. "These star-peerers, what do they know? Are their eyes better than mine? Can they shoot springbucks better than I can? Don't I see that the sun gets up every morning *there*" (he pointed to the east), "and don't I see every evening that it goes down *there*?"

He shook the long stick towards the west, as though threatening an astronomer with the consequences of his folly.

"Ja, Oom; but you see it's this way—"

"Ach! don't tell me about your this way and that way. You find me a star-peerer who knows his Bible or has better eyes than I have, and I'll listen to him. Doesn't the Bible say that Joshua told the sun to stand still? Doesn't the Prophet Isaiah say that the Lord stretched the sky over the earth like a tent? These star-peerers are all rogues and Romanist heathens."

"But, Oom," said the cattle-dealer, who was, as it were, blowing the fuse of a torpedo which he had in reserve, "how is it that these star-peerers are able to tell long before the times when the sun and the moon will be darkened?"

"How are they able to tell? Why, they find it out from the almanack, of course." The only almanack with which the Trek-Boer is acquainted is one issued by the Dutch Reformed Church. This document is adorned with the Signs of the Zodiac, and is heavily garnished with Scripture texts. It is believed by certain classes of the Boers that the almanack is annually deduced from the Bible by a committee of Church ministers.

The cattle-dealer, blown up—to change the old metaphor—by his own torpedo, had to own himself vanquished. Old Schalk's reputation for wisdom rose higher than ever, and a deadly blow was dealt to the heliocentric theory in Bushmanland.

The lovers strolled away over the sandy plain, which was now covered with a rich carpet of variously hued flowers. Gorgeous gazanias of the tint of the richest mahogany, and with the base of each petal eyed like a peacock's tail; blue, sweet-scented heliophilas, purple and crimson mesembryanthemums, and lovely variegated pelargoniums brushed their feet at every step. They said little to one another, and that little could interest none but themselves. Both were ignorant and illiterate to a degree; their range of ideas was more limited than it is easy to describe, or even to realise; but their hearts were young and full of vague, sweet, unutterable thoughts. The springbucks—the advance detachment of a large "trek"—were scattered, singly or in small groups, over the illimitable plain. They sheered off, feeding tamely, to either side. The meerkats scuttled back to their low, burrow-pierced mounds, where they sat erect on a tripod, formed by hind legs and tail, ready to dart underground. The striped-faced gemsbuck-mice dashed wildly into their burrows in terror, and then out again in uncontrollable curiosity.

As they walked homeward in the short gloaming Max asked Susannah if she would always be true, even if her people were against him and his brother drove him away. The girl looked straight into his eyes and answered "Yes," in a clear, low tone. Max, believing her, saw Hope shining through the clouds of uncertainty that filled the future, and was happy.

When they reached the camp the short Desert twilight had nearly faded and the eastern stars were burning brightly. The gathering had dispersed, and Old Schalk, sitting smoking in his chair before the mat-house, was the only person visible.

"Well," he said, "what is this they tell me about you and my niece?"

"I want to marry her, Uncle; I am very fond of her."

"Marry her? You will have to become a Christian before you marry *my* niece?"

This was meant sarcastically. No Boer believes in the possibility of a Jew becoming a Christian.

"Yes, Uncle, I'll do that at once."

"Hear him, now. He thinks a Jew can become a Christian as easily as a man can change his shirt. Did you ever hear of a jackal turning into a tame dog in a day?" Max flushed hotly but made no reply. "I never heard of such a thing in all my life," continued the old Boer. "It is not even as if you were rich and had a shop of your own; but you are only a poor little boy without anything. Look here, I do not want your brother Nathan to think that I have had anything to do with this foolishness."

Just then a diminutive Hottentot approached from behind the camp, saluted Old Schalk, and squatted down on the ground close by upon his hams. The man was clad in a few ragged skins and looked weak and emaciated.

"Well, schepsel, where do you come from?"

"Out of the veld, Baas."

"And where are you going to?"

"I have come to the Baas."

"For what?"

"I have come to the Baas to look for work."

"Ja, and what is your name?"

"I am old Gert Gemsbok, Baas."

"What! Are you the vagabond Bushman who got Willem Bester into the tronk?"

"I am he, Baas."

"And you come to ask me to give you work?"

"I only told the truth, Baas."

"Ach, what does a Bushman know about truth?"

"If I did a sin when I spoke the truth, Baas, I have had my punishment: for six long years I have lived like a badger in a hole. I am a human being, Baas; let me come back and live among other human beings."

"No, no, schepsel; not a Boer in Bushmanland will give you work. Willem Bester died in the tronk. No, no!"

"I have a sickly old wife, Baas, and she cannot live any longer on the veld-kost. Give me work, Baas, and I will serve you faithfully."

"No, no, schepsel; go back and live with the badgers."

Max heard and wondered. His awakening soul was shocked at the unreasoning cruelty of the old Boer's conduct. The Hottentot had arisen slowly and feebly from the ground and was walking away; the young Jew followed and soon overtook him. Max had been bartering fat-tailed sheep for goods with some of his customers and he wanted a herd. He told Gert Gemsbok to follow him to the shop.

That night the old Hottentot told his tale, or most of it, to Max. They sat up in the shop until late, Gemsbok happy in the enjoyment of a pipeful of good tobacco. He had lacked the means of smoking ever since he had been driven into banishment. The suffering which this deprivation must have entailed can only be realised by those who know the Hottentot's dependence upon his pipe.

Max burned with wrath at what he heard; his ingenuous soul revolted at the tale of injustice and stupid cruelty. By instinct he could tell that the old man's story was ingenuous and, so far as it went, unreserved. He called to mind that Old Schalk had not attempted to deny Gemsbok's plea that the evidence given by him against Willem Bester was true.

Max engaged Gemsbok at a salary of eight shillings per month, with rations for himself. This was a fair rate of remuneration for Bushmanland. The work which the old Hottentot had to do was to look after the flock of three hundred fat-tailed sheep which Max had recently acquired, to herd them all day in the Desert, and to haul water for them with a derrick out of the well when he drove them home every night. Gemsbok knew that he could every day gather enough veld-kost to supplement his ration and make it suffice for his wife as well as for himself. He had left her under a bush a few miles away. Before daylight next morning he was well on his course to fetch her, with hope and gladness filling his heart.

The Gemsbok *ménage* was established in a cleft of the kopje-side about fifty yards behind the store. The habitation consisted of a movable screen of loose bushes about two feet high and shaped like a crescent. This was shifted from one side to another of the fireplace as the wind changed. A vagrant dog which Gert had found far out in the Desert, half-famished for want of water, was added to the strength of the establishment, and became the devoted slave of its rescuer.

The old couple now tasted happiness probably far greater than any they had previously experienced. Max was kind to them. Presents of old sacks and a few articles of cast-off clothing, fragments of food from his scanty table, an occasional pinch of tobacco,—such things filled the hearts of these belated creatures with deep joy and thankfulness. A pot of salve for the old woman's legs was provided, and the result was satisfactory.

Max found Gert a most intelligent and entertaining companion, and mentally far in advance of any of the inhabitants of the Desert whom he had met. The old man's experiences had been varied and his life full of the tragic, and he seemed not to have forgotten anything he had ever seen or heard in the course of his long struggles against adverse Fate.

The ramkee was much in evidence. Oom Schulpad, with a true artist's generous appreciation of the art of a fellow craftsman, often brought his violin to the shop at night. There the two musicians would contend, like two troubadours, in a kind of tournament of song. Sometimes they would play duets, and it was then that Gemsbok proved his skill, for he accompanied without difficulty any air played upon the violin after he had heard it once. He would sit and listen attentively whilst Oom Schulpad played it slowly over. Then the notes of the ramkee would second the more civilised instrument as truly as if the music lay printed before the player and he could read it.

On the night when this occurred for the first time, after Gemsbok had returned to his scherm, Oom Schulpad sat silently on the counter for a few minutes. Then, as he took his departure he said, in a musing tone—

"Ja, he knows more music than I, that old Bushman."

As Gemsbok's poor old wife was entirely helpless, it was he who fetched, wood and water and attended to all the domestic duties. The old woman slept most of the day, but at night the cheerful firelight from the scherm lit up the kopjes long after the last of the Boers lay snoring. Then the old couple would sit, toasting themselves at the cheerful blaze, and chatting happily together, except when some lively tune from the ramkee startled the ancient silence of the Desert.

One of the Boers camped nearest the shop was a man named Koos Bester, cousin of the Willem Bester who had died in prison after being sentenced upon old Gemsbok's evidence. Koos was a very big, sallow, dark-haired man with a scraggy fringe of coarse, black beard around his chin, and eyes of a very peculiar shade of light grey. His usual mien was melancholy, his strength was prodigious, his hands and feet were of enormous size and looked as if they belonged to some one else.

Koos Bester was a man who seldom either spoke or smiled; nevertheless he could hardly be called morose. He was by no means a bad fellow in his way, and was devotedly attached to his comely wife and his three small children. His father-in-law, a very old man, lived with him. The Besters usually camped at a water-place on the other side of the dunes. As, however, no rain had fallen in that vicinity for some time, they moved over to Namies, meaning to return to the spot they had come to regard as their home as soon as circumstances permitted.

Koos had been much attached to his cousin Willem and had felt the latter's imprisonment and death very keenly. He hated the sight of Gert Gemsbok, who continually reminded him of Willem's fate; the very fact of knowing that the old Hottentot was in the neighbourhood was sufficient to make him miserable. One day he asked Max to dismiss Gemsbok, but Max indignantly refused.

The scherm was in full view of the Besters' camp, and the sight of the cheerful camp-fire with the old couple sitting next to it was a nightly affront. Then the ramkee got upon Koos' nerves to such an extent that he became very unhappy indeed. Gert's tune, with its endless variations, became absolutely hateful to the melancholy Boer. One day, in the course of a discussion on the subject, Koos had the bad taste to insult Oom Schulpad by a reference to his physical defects. The old fiddler had spoken in terms of admiration of the Hottentot's skill as a musician, and Koos lost his temper. Oom Schulpad said nothing at the time, but he scored up a grudge against Koos. Whenever Oom Schulpad felt that he owed another anything in this way, he took a pride in devising means to pay the debt.

At length Koos found that he could stand the ramkee no longer, so he shifted his camp to the other side of the kopjes, where the tune could not reach his disgusted ears. A few days afterwards a thunderstorm passed over the eastern fringe of the dunes, and he returned to his favourite camping-place. But Gert Gemsbok's air haunted him for weeks with deadly persistency.

Chapter Seven.

How Jan Roster was Twice Interrupted.

One day four sleek mules drawing a light buggy came trotting along the sandy road from the southward to Namies. In the vehicle were sitting Jan Roster and his half-breed servant, Piet Noona. They came from that part of Bushmanland in which no European can dwell, on account of the extreme brackishness of the water—from an area the only inhabitants of which are a few dozen families of half-breeds, who live by poaching wild ostriches in defiance of the law. These people are very like human red-herrings in appearance—probably from the amount of salt which they constantly imbibe.

The right of occupation of the district had been leased by Roster from Government, and he, in turn, sublet his rights to the half-breeds. The rent was paid in ostrich feathers; these the landlord collected himself, and took over at his own price.

The unique method practised by these people in hunting the ostrich may be worth describing shortly. The ostrich runs probably swifter than any other description of game. It has, however, one peculiarity—if kept moving, even with comparative slowness, for more than a couple of hours on a hot day, it gets heat-apoplexy, and suddenly dies. The manner of its dying under these circumstances is peculiar. It drops in its tracks, rolls over three times upon the sand, turns on its back and expires, with legs extended vertically.

The half-breeds sent out boys mounted on ponies, sometimes for a distance of seventy or eighty miles, into the Desert. These start in two parties, each taking a different direction. After reaching ground where, from the spoor, it can be seen that ostriches abound, the two parties converge towards each other, leaving, at intervals, individuals stationary at certain points. A chain, the links of which are several miles long, is thus formed around a large space, into the centre of which all the ostriches which it contains are gradually coaxed. As soon as the cordon is complete, the birds are started at a run towards the saltpans, where the camps of the half-breeds are. As the horses of the hunters actually engaged in chasing become exhausted, their places are taken by others waiting along the wide-apart lines, between which the hapless birds are being driven. After a time the birds begin to drop, one by one. The hunters who made the running at the beginning, and who now come slowly along on the spoor of the chase, pick the carcases up, one by one. Then the feathers are carefully plucked out and tied in bundles, whilst the meat is cut from the bones and hung across the saddles of the weary horses.

Jan Roster's buggy was of unusual make. It had a skeleton frame, and, where the well ought to have been under the seat, was fitted an ample tin case, which could be easily unshipped. The reason of this was well known to every Trek-Boer in Bushmanland. The box was the receptacle of the feathers collected as rent from the half-breeds, and, in the rare event of Jan's meeting a policeman or the Special Magistrate upon his rounds, it could be slipped off and buried in the sand. Once he had reached home with his collections Jan felt himself quite safe. He farmed tame ostriches himself, and the possession of the feathers could always be accounted for as being the result of legitimate pluckings.

Jan's tin box was full of feathers as he drove up to Namies, but this fact did not cause him the least embarrassment. He pulled up within a few yards of Old Schalk's camp, and, while Piet Noona was outspanning the mules, he untied the tin box and carried it at once into the mat-house. From the way in which he did this, it could be seen that he had evidently done the same kind of thing before. He knew that he ran no risk of being betrayed—"Hawks dinna pyke out hawks' een."

It was Saturday afternoon when Jan arrived; he was soon sitting in the mat-house drinking coffee, munching Boer biscuit, and glancing tenderly at Susannah from time to time. Maria and Petronella sat on the big bed giggling, whispering together, and nudging one another.

Mrs Hattingh, exhausted by the heat, was sitting near the door fanning her perspiring face with her cappie.

Susannah's countenance shone with a new light which made it very good to look upon. Ever since her engagement she had become much neater and more tasteful in her dress. In this respect she had always been in strong contrast to her cousins, who, in spite of their taste for pronounced colours, were utter slatterns. To-day they were dressed out in finery of a distressing type. Maria wore a new light-pink cashmere dress, a purple-flowered cappie, and around her neck a dark-blue handkerchief. Petronella's frock was light blue, her kerchief was scarlet, and her cappie was of the same kind as her sister's. Both sisters wore white cotton stockings and new veldschoens—the latter just finished for the occasion by Oom Schulpad. The dresses were made of the material which had been obtained upon Mrs Hattingh's fraudulent representations to the effect that it was required for Susannah.

There was a reason for all this splendour of attire. Maria and Petronella had just made a double conquest, and the double-conquered were immediately expected to call. These were two young men who had recently come to Namies on a courting expedition, from eastern Bushmanland. They came, saw, and succumbed, all within the space of a week. They had not yet declared themselves, but were expected to do so that afternoon. These two hunted in a couple; one never came without the other, and they did not feel the slightest embarrassment in making love ardently in each other's immediate neighbourhood.

It was about the middle of the afternoon when the expected swains arrived. Both were tall, loose-jointed young men. They had been to the shop and there purchased suits of "reach-me-downs" of distressing texture, pattern, and cut, as well as flabby-rimmed "smasher" hats. They had rather vacant faces, with good-natured expressions. Christoffel (commonly called "Stoffel") van Lell, Maria's admirer, wore a tweed coat, which was much too small for him, and the sleeves of which severally revealed half a foot of red, bony wrist.

His trousers were of brown corduroy of the most fragrant quality. Willem Henrico, the willing slave of Petronella's charms, wore a suit of Bedford cord, the jacket of which was double-breasted and adorned with white delft buttons as large as cheese-plates. New veldschoens and cheap, glittering spurs adorned their extensive feet. Spurs serve as a sort of trade-flag in courting on the high plains; a young man with a new pair is known to be in search of a wife.

A walk was proposed. This Mrs Hattingh agreed to with the proviso that the road over the plains was taken and strictly adhered to, and that the couples kept close together. The young men wanted to wander among the kopjes, and the girls seemed to approve of that route. Mrs Hattingh, however, was inexorable. When she emphatically repeated her injunction about keeping close together, Maria said, deprecatingly: "Ach, Ou' Ma," (Ou' Ma, grandmother) and pouted. Susannah flatly refused to go, although Jan's request that she should do so was ostentatiously seconded by Mrs Hattingh. Jan, accordingly, decided to remain at the camp, so the other couples started by themselves.

Mrs Hattingh soon afterwards stood up and waddled to the scherm, leaving Jan and Susannah alone together. Old Schalk was sitting in his chair on the other side of the wagon, in the shade.

Jan became very nervous. After a few minutes he got up hesitatingly, and moved his chair close to the little cross-legged stool on which Susannah was sitting. He cleared his throat several times before he could force himself to speak. Susannah was pale, but quite unembarrassed. She regarded her unwelcome admirer with eyes that had a wicked snap in them, and he became demoralised under her disdain.

In vain did he speak of his house, his flocks, his horses, and the places he had seen—not to mention the important people with whom he was on terms of intimacy. None of these things moved Susannah. Her hands were closed into two shapely little fists—so tightly that there was not a vestige of blood to be seen in the knuckles. Jan ought to have noticed her hands, and taken warning accordingly, but he rushed blindly upon his fate.

"Susannah," he said, beseechingly, "I have come a long way to see you."

"So? Was that why you brought the tin box?"

He floundered; in spite of the practice he had had, proposing was difficult. Besides, Susannah's last remark was not calculated to set him at his ease.

"Are you not glad to see me, Susannah?"

"Why should I be?"

"Well, I—you see—I wanted to tell you about my new house."

"What have I to do with houses? I live in a mat-house."

"But wouldn't you like to live in a big house with rooms, and a stoep, and a harmonium inside, and furniture brought all the way from Clanwilliam?"

Susannah's thoughts wandered. In a dreamy tone she replied—

"I don't know; perhaps I might."

Jan took this for a sign of yielding. He bent over and passed his arm around the girl's waist.

Susannah's dreaming was over. She sprang up and, in the act of doing so, swung round and dealt Jan a swinging blow on the ear with her small, but firm and nervous fist. Jan felt as if the thunders of the Apocalypse had discharged themselves over his left shoulder. He put his hand up to the side of his head to ascertain whether his ear was still there or had been burnt off. Susannah had hurt her hand so much that the tears started in her eyes. However, she managed to escape from the mat-house without showing her distress.

Jan, very much crestfallen and with a bad singing in the left side of his head, strolled away among the other camps. He could see, far out on the plains, the two double dots which indicated the respective pairs of lovers, and the spectacle made him sigh with envy. As the violent pain in his ear calmed down to a sensation more like that of being gently roasted, he began to make excuses for Susannah. Perhaps, he thought, he had been too precipitate. At all events he would go back to tea, Mrs Hattingh having invited him to do so.

When Jan returned at dusk he found van Lell and Henrico sitting on the big cartel bed in the mat-house—the nuptial couch of Old Schalk—with their arms around the waists of their respective charmers. On each of the four faces was an expression of fatuous bliss. The lovers took not the least notice of Old Schalk or Mrs Hattingh, or, for the matter of that, of Jan himself.

At table the lovers did not allow their affections to prevent their all making excellent suppers. The expected proposals had been duly made that afternoon. During the meal each of the affianced maidens passed little tit-bits into her lover's mouth with her own fair fingers from time to time. These were munched with expressions of rapture by the recipients. Susannah was still indignant, and glanced at Jan from time to time in a manner that made him lose his appetite. The pain in her hand had lasted longer than that in Jan's ear; of course she blamed him exclusively for the hurt.

After supper another walk was proposed, but this was uncompromisingly vetoed by Mrs Hattingh. Max came in later, and, as usual, sat down as far from every one as possible. Jan wondered at the black looks which the visitor got from the old couple. By and by, however, Susannah brought her little stool close to where Max was sitting, and then a glimmering of the true state of affairs came to Jan. The pain seemed to come back to his ear with renewed intensity. Ere long he found he could stand the strain no longer, so he said, "Goodnight," and rose to depart. In response to a question from Old Schalk, he said that he would hold a religious service on the following day.

Next morning at about ten o'clock there was a considerable gathering of Boers at the Hattingh camp. Stout, frowsy "tantas" and portly "ooms" strolled up with dignity or waddled laboriously through the sand. Gaudily arrayed maidens followed with their attendant swains. A general requisition for stools and benches, had been made, and these were arranged in a semicircle in front of the wagon. The children of the congregation sat on the ground where sheepskins had been stretched at the feet of the elders. Old Schalk's chair was placed apart, immediately below the wagon-box, in a position from which he could note the effect of the exhortations on the faces of the others. The service began with a psalm sung after the fashion followed in the Scotch kirks of a century ago—very slowly, and much through the nose. Old Schalk followed with a prayer, which might be described as so much denunciation of people in general, clothed in the phraseology of the Prophet Jeremiah, when the utterer of the Lamentations was most exercised over the sins of Israel. There was a rumour afloat to the effect that the Government was about to tax the Trek-Boers to some slight extent, in proportion to the number of stock they depastured in Bushmanland, so Old Schalk was the mouthpiece of the general indignation.

The prayer over, Jan Roster mounted the wagon-box and began his sermon. His text was a wide one—it embraced the whole of the Ten Commandments. In an unctuous and impassioned manner he fulminated against all sorts and conditions of transgressors. Some of the Commandments he slurred over—others he expounded at great length. When he reached the fourth he glanced menacingly at Max, who stood outside the circle, opposite where Susannah was sitting. The breaking of the Sabbath was, according to Jan, the root of all evil. He called upon the legislators of the land to impose the heaviest penalties for all contraventions of the Divine ordinance on the subject. He spoke in the most opprobrious terms of the Jews, who, out of the wickedness of their unregenerate hearts, desecrated this most holy day, and kept Saturday as a day of devotion in its stead. He, Jan, was a sinner, but among all the faults which his conscience laid to his charge, Sabbath-breaking was not to be found. No, he had always kept holy the Lord's day—never travelled on it—never attended to worldly concerns between midnight on Saturday and the morning of Monday.

Just then an interruption came. Piet Noona, Jan's driver and confidential servant, forced his way along the side of the wagon until he reached the front wheel, just over which Jan was holding forth from the wagon-box.

"Baas, Baas!" said he, in an agitated whisper. Jan glanced down with displeasure in his eye, frowned, shook his head, and proceeded to the discussion of the fifth commandment Piet, however, was not to be put off. He caught hold of the leg of Jan's trousers between his finger and thumb, and began to tug at it.

"Baas, Baas!" said he again, in a tone almost of agony.

"Go away—wait until I have finished," said Jan, in an irritated whisper.

"Baas, Baas!" reiterated Piet, in a whisper which could be heard by all the congregation, "die Magistrate zijn wa' kom aan." ("The Magistrate's wagon is approaching.")

Jan reeled and staggered as if he had received a blow. Then he bent down towards the agitated Piet and whispered hysterically the word "Inspan!"

Piet darted off. From the curt and summary way in which Jan dealt with the remaining Commandments one might have thought that they were of comparatively little importance. He brought the service to a close in almost indecent haste, and then dived from the wagon-box behind the canvas curtain, in front of which he had been holding forth. From there he rushed to the mat-house, whence he emerged in an incredibly short space of time, carrying the box of feathers. This he ran with to the buggy. He shoved it under the seat, and over it he draped a sheepskin kaross with ostentatious carelessness. In a few minutes the astonished congregation, which had scattered into interested groups, was scandalised at seeing Jan Roster, the strict

Sabbatarian, disappear in a dusty cloud on the road which led southward through the Desert.

However, Jan had got safely away with his tin box and its incriminating contents, and there was not the slightest fear of any of the Boers giving information to the authorities on the subject.

The Spedai Magistrate's wagon brought the Namies mail from Kenhardt. The mail consisted of three letters—two of which were for Max—and a few circular advertisements from enterprising promoters of patent medicines.

Max's letters filled him with joy. One was from his brother Nathan, saying he had made so successful a trip—having secured a large quantity of feathers of the very best quality—that he had decided to visit Cape Town for the purpose of disposing of his spoils and buying a fresh stock of "negotie," or trading truck. Consequently he did not intend returning for about another six weeks.

Nathan gave minute directions upon many points connected with the management of the business—more especially with reference to the giving of credit to the Boers, who, as he knew, would soon be collecting at Namies in considerable numbers. The Hattingh account was, if possible, to be closed at once; in no case was any more credit to be given in that direction. Max sighed with deep relief. After the daily dread of Nathan's arrival which had overshadowed him for so many weary weeks, this long respite seemed like a prospective eternity.

The other letter bore a foreign post-mark. It was from a notary in Hamburg, informing him that an uncle, of whose very name he had but a faint recollection, had recently died and left him a legacy of about 150 pounds. It seemed a fortune. Why, with that sum he could open a store for himself, as large as the one he was managing on a pittance for another. What a relief it was to find himself independent of Nathan—to realise that there was now some prospect of his being able to make a home for Susannah.

Chapter Eight.

The Trek-Bokken.

The great annual "trek" of springbucks began, and Namies fell into a state of ferment. For about a week small droves of bucks had been seen passing to the westward. One morning clouds of dust were noticed arising into a windless sky about ten miles away to the south. By this it was known that the "trek" had really begun, and that the drove of game was passing unusually far to the northward. Within an hour after sunrise the Wagons were emptied of their contents, whilst every male of European descent above the age of ten was furbishing up a gun.

All sorts and conditions of firearms were to be seen, from the flint-lock of three-quarters of a century ago to the modern Martini and Express.

Breakfast over, the wagons, drawn by teams of oxen which had been standing in the yoke since early morning, moved off towards different points on the trek-line. No horses were taken; a waterless country was now to be entered, and a horse becomes useless in hot weather after a day and a half without water. On the other hand, an ox can endure thirst for a week without becoming incapable of work.

Each wagon carried a couple of small kegs of water, a pillow-case full of Boer biscuits, a small bag of ground coffee, and a kettle. The more luxuriously inclined among the hunters took with them karosses, made of the skins of fat-tailed sheep, to lie under at night. The majority, however, took nothing whatever in the way of bedding.

As the wagons cleared the circle of low kopjes it could be seen that the trek was an unusually large one. As far as the eye could range from north-east to south-west the horizon was obscured by rising clouds of dust. Here and there in the immense vista, a particularly dense cloud could be seen ascending slowly. This indicated a locality where a mob of more than average compactness was pressing westward, impelled by the strange trek instinct.

Old Schalk was a keen sportsman—as that term is understood among the Trek-Boers. In fact the "trek-bokken" were the only things he ever got very excited about. Sitting in his chair—which had been tied in the wagon—and accompanied by a youth whom he had provided with an old gun and some ammunition, and who had agreed to give up half of what he shot in payment, he was drawn towards the trek as fast as a fresh span of oxen could go with the almost empty wagon. Besides his gun Old Schalk took two large "slacht eizers," or iron traps—cruel things with toothed iron jaws that would smash the leg of a horse.

As the wagons approached the immense drove the dust began to die down, for the tired bucks had paused for their regular rest during the heat of the day. Far away could be seen dense white masses, between which light-coloured dots were thickly sprinkled.

The springbuck is pure white on the belly and flanks, and has a mane of long, white, hair extending from the root of the tail to the shoulders. This mane is usually concealed to a great extent by the fawn-coloured ridges of hair between which it lies. It can, however, be erected at will to about five inches in height, and extended to about six inches in breadth. The sides of the animal are a light fawn colour, upon which lies a horizontal stripe of dark brown about two and a half inches in width and extending from the shoulder to the flank. The horns, shaped like the classic lyre, are about eight inches in length, and are ringed to within a couples of inches of the tip. The animal stands about two feet nine inches in height at the shoulder, and weighs about ninety pounds when fully grown.

Seen at a distance, or when the sun is shining against them, the springbucks appear to be white all over. It is in the early morning, or when running away from or in circles around a bewildered dog—deceived into the idea that it is about to succeed in catching the lissom quarry—that the springbucks are seen at their best, and in their most characteristic attitudes and movements. Then the spine becomes arched until the nose almost touches the ground, the mane of long, stiff, white hair expands laterally, whilst every fibre stands erect and apart. As the animal careers along with the appearance of a bounding disc, its feet are drawn together and it sways, like a skater, first to one side and then to the other—some times to an angle of thirty degrees from the vertical.

There is something inexpressibly sad about the fate of these hapless creatures. Beautiful as anything that breathes, destructive as locusts, they are preyed upon by man and brute in the illimitable wilderness—even as the great shoals of fish are preyed upon by their enemies in the illimitable ocean. The unbounded Desert spaces, apparently meant for their inheritance, hold for them no sanctuary; the hyaena and the jackal hang and batten on the skirts of their helpless host; the vultures wheel above its rear and tear the eyes out of the less vigorous which lag behind. Sportsman and pot-hunter, Boer, half-breed and Bushman, beast of the burrow and bird of the air, slaughter their myriads; but still the mighty mass assembles every year and surges across the Desert like a tempest in its travail of torture. Why should all this loveliness and symmetry have been created in such lavish prodigality only to be extinguished by a slow process of agony and violent death?

For if there be any design anywhere in Nature's so-called "Plan," the Desert was meant to be the inheritance of these animals. They were developed under its conditions, its sparse and tardy products are for them all-sufficing; they were in harmony with their ungracious environment until man came to disturb the balance. The semi-civilised human beings who are superseding the springbucks are, physically, and, *pari passu* mentally, deteriorating under the conditions subject to which the latter flourished.

Within a measurable time the lyre-shaped horns strewn thickly over the veld will be the sole remaining sign of a vanished race, for the springbuck will inevitably become extinct in Bushmanland, as the bison has become extinct in the North American prairies.

The "trek" is due to the instinct which impels the does to drop their young somewhere upon the eastern fringe of the Desert, which extends, north and south, for several hundred miles. This fringe is the limit of the western rains. These fall between April and September, when the Desert is at its driest, and bring out the green herbage necessary for the new-born fawns.

As the area over which the bucks range becomes more and more circumscribed, the trek, although the number of bucks is rapidly diminishing, becomes more and more destructive, owing to its greater concentration. The fawning season over, the herd melts slowly and flows gradually westward, until some night distant flashes of lightning on the cloudless horizon indicate where—perhaps hundreds of miles away—the first thunderstorm of the season is labouring down from where its bolts were forged in the far, tropical north. Next morning not a single buck will be visible—all will have vanished like ghosts, making for the distant track of the rain.

The wagons were drawn for some little distance into the course of the drove, and halted a few miles apart. Then the oxen were unyoked and driven back towards Namies.

Immediately there began a great and ruthless slaughter. Whilst trekking the bucks are very easy to shoot; in fact, if the trek be a large one there is no sport involved in killing them, for they press blindly on, only sheering off slightly to avoid an enemy. They become bewildered in strange surroundings; their only impulse is to surge forward in a flood-tide of destruction and beauty.

From right and left could be heard the dropping shots—some far away and some near—each the death-knell of one of the loveliest of created things. The Boers had crept out for some distance from the wagons, and each had taken up what he considered a favourable position. Here he cleared a circular space about ten feet in diameter by pulling the karoo-bushes, roots and all, out of the sand. The bushes were then piled around the space cleared until a low, inconspicuous fence, about nine inches in height, was formed, the root-ends of the bushes lying inwards.

At nightfall the herd suddenly began to move on once more, in obedience to some mysteriously communicated impulse. All night long the muffled thunder of their hoofs could be heard, whilst clouds of dust hung motionless in the dew-damp air. Now and then the faint shock of a distant gun discharge could be distinguished above the sound of the trampling. In their mad career some of the larger and more consolidated troops would rush to within a few yards of a wagon before they became aware of its presence. Then the mass would open out slightly and flow onwards in a divided stream, which, however, would reunite a few yards farther on. On occasions such as this the Boers or their Hottentot servants would shoot into the dense multitude, sometimes killing or wounding three or four bucks at one shot.

Old Schalk now set a trap at each side of the wagon, and the Hottentots had to get up several times in the night to cut the throats of the captured animals and reset the engines.

Early in the morning the wagons were sent back to Namies loaded with the slaughtered game. Late in the afternoon they returned empty, to go back again on the following morning with a fresh load.

For three days and nights the trek was at its height; then no more dense troops were to be seen. For a week or more, however, plenty of profitable shooting could be had at the stragglers.

At Namies the Boer women and children were busy cutting up the carcases and converting the meat into "bultong." From each haunch the bone was removed, whilst the meat which lay thick along the back where the ribs join the spine was cut out in long strips. All the meat was then slightly sprinkled with salt and left to lie in heaps for twenty-four hours. After this it was hung for a few days upon lines slung between the ribs of the mat-houses and the laths of the wagon-tents. Then, if the sun did not shine too fiercely, it would be hung out in the open.

After a few weeks of such treatment the "bultong" is fit for use, and if stored in a dry place may be kept for an indefinite time. This

Behind this fence the hunter lay prone, peering over it now and then to mark the approach of the game, which wandered aimlessly about, singly or in small groups. Whenever a buck approached to within a few yards of the scherm, the occupant, with unerring aim, would send a bullet through some vital part, and the animal would fall, its companions scattering, often only to get within range of another scherm. The karoo-bushes grow to a height of about a foot; consequently the dead bucks were usually concealed from view. If one lay unduly revealed, the hunter would creep out and strew a few bushes over it, thus hiding it effectually.

At evening the Hottentot servants drove in the oxen, inspanned them to the wagons, and drove out to the various scherms for the purpose of bringing back the game to the different camping-places. The carcases were then split down in front and laid open in the cool night air.

Old Schalk, on account of his weak legs, was conveyed by wagon right to the spot where he decided to establish his scherm; then the wagon moved back for a couple of miles and the oxen were outspanned. He laid himself down comfortably in his scherm, where he kept a Hottentot boy to attend him. Under his large body was a sheepskin kaross, for he believed in doing his shooting, like everything else, comfortably. The two terrible traps were brought into requisition. By means of the united exertions of Old Schalk and the Hottentot the springs were forced back and the frightful jaws laid open. Then the traps were carried out and carefully set, one on each side, and half buried in the loose sand. They were placed each about a hundred yards away from the scherm, and a troop of bucks would sometimes pass over one or other of the intervening spaces. Under ordinary circumstances no buck would tread upon so unusual looking an object. At a shot, however, the frightened creatures would spring into the air in different directions, and in the confusion one would perhaps alight on the engine. Then the horrible jaws would snap, and the poor animal, held by the sinews of a shattered limb, would roll over and over on the sand, bellowing in agony.

substance forms the staple animal food of the Trek-Boer for the greater part of the year.

The skins were pegged out on the ground to dry; then they were stowed away in heaps, afterwards to be "brayed" soft, sewn into mats, and bartered to the Jew hawkers.

Chapter Nine.

The Last of the "Old Woman."

Max had no taste for slaughter. The hunter's instinct, which makes so many otherwise humane men cruel, was not in him. He therefore felt it no privation that he was unable to leave the shop and join the hunters as he had done in previous years when the trek had taken place. On the other hand he felt with satisfaction that he could now see more of Susannah, her uncle being out of the way, and he made the most of his opportunities in this respect.

Max was rapidly developing from a boy into a man, and many of the little traits specially characteristic of modern Israel began to show themselves in him. Of Old Schalk he stood in awe; the brutal directness of the way in which the old Boer uttered all his thoughts frightened him. Mrs Hattingh, however, had ceased to impress him since the day she had obtained the dresses for her granddaughters fraudulently and on the strength of his attachment to Susannah. Max felt that he held her at a moral disadvantage, and she tacitly acquiesced in this.

Max spent every evening while Old Schalk was away at his sweetheart's side. He told her of his legacy, and around this nucleus they began to weave plans for the future. Max had saved a little money out of the small salary which his brother allowed him. He thought seriously of leaving Nathan's service as soon as the latter returned, and setting up on his own account as a hawker.

His first notion was to buy some stock and set up as a Trek-Boer, but Susannah put a decided veto upon this proposal. The prospect of being married to a man who spent most of his life in wandering about with a cart and four donkeys was almost equally unattractive. The latter alternative might, however, lead to something better eventually. Susannah was in no hurry; she told her lover plainly that although she was prepared to wait indefinitely for him she would not marry until he could give her a proper home.

Late one night, after Max had returned home to the shop, he heard a knock at the door. He found Gert Gemsbok standing before the threshold. The old Hottentot stepped in, and, as usual, sat down on the floor.

"Baas Max, I want to tell you a secret."

"Yes; what is it?"

"Baas Max, when I was living down on the bank of the river I one day picked something up."

"Yes; what was it?"

"You have been kind to me and I can trust you. Here is what I picked up."

Gemsbok handed over to Max the smallest of the six diamonds. He had, after careful consideration, determined to trust his master so far, with the view of realising part at least of his valuables.

Max took the stone and looked carefully at it. He knew well enough that it was a rough diamond; as a child in Cape Town he had often seen illicitly obtained stones of this kind handed round among the Jews who frequented the lodging-house where he stayed for a short time upon his arrival in the colony. The gem weighed about eight carats; it was of good water and perfect shape.

"I found it," continued Gemsbok, "hidden in a boot which came down in the flood, just above the Augrabies Falls. I know, for I have worked at the diamond fields, that I should be sent back to the tronk if that stone were found on me, so I thought you might sell it and give me half the money. If you will do this it will satisfy me."

Max considered for a while, and then decided that this was a matter for his brother to deal with. He knew well enough that the possession of diamonds which could not be satisfactorily accounted for was a criminal offence severely punishable. The law was to Max a thing very dreadful. He had never seen its manifestations, but he had heard of Willem Bester and others who had broken the law and suffered grievously in consequence. Nathan, however, as was proved in his ostrich-feather dealings, held the law in sovereign contempt. Nathan was the man to deal with a matter such as this; Max would have none of it. In the meantime, however, he agreed to keep the stone in the small iron safe and to advance Gemsbok some coffee, sugar, and tobacco, for the delectation of himself and his "Old Woman," as the latter always called her, upon its security.

But the "Old Woman" had no long enjoyment of the luxuries, for two days later, when Gemsbok came in from the veld with his flock, he found that she was dead. She had passed away in her sleep. Gemsbok expressed himself to Max as being glad that the poor old creature had breathed her last. She had, he said, suffered so much of late, and now she would never feel pain or privation any more. He dug a hole in a sandy gully behind one of the smaller kopjes and there the poor, unlovely corpse was laid. In spite of her physical sufferings the quaint old creature had spent a very happy time at Namies. She had enjoyed a sufficiency of fairly wholesome food, besides the occasional trifles in the way of coffee, sugar, and tobacco which Max's bounty supplied her with. These had afforded her the keenest and, perhaps, the only enjoyment she was capable of feeling.

Gemsbok, in spite of his repeated declarations that he was glad the "Old Woman" was gone, did not appear to be happy. No matter how bright the fire of candle-bushes, the scherm was lonely at night—even an old woman so broken down by rheumatism and poverty of blood that she could not use her limbs and was hardly capable of carrying her food to her mouth, was better than no human companion at all.

Gemsbok had now no companion but his dog, which was an animal as friendless as its master. All day long alone in the veld, under the changeless Desert sky; all night long alone in the scherm, under the unregarding stars. Man is a gregarious animal, and the burthen of one's own presence galls as only those burthens do which carry as dead weight the broken shackles of one of Nature's disregarded laws.

Sleep was difficult to get. It had been usual for the old couple to remain awake talking half the night through. Lying awake alone proved to be a very different thing. He moved his scherm to another spot; that did not improve matters, so he moved it back again. He no longer enjoyed his coffee or tobacco. The average man almost invariably gets to love anything totally dependent on him—no matter how unlovely it may be. Some loves are not recognised in anything like their fulness until the removal of the thing loved leaves a void which can never be filled.

A Hottentot is naturally among the most sociable of beings; Gert Gemsbok was no exception to the rule of his race in this respect. He had, however, made no friends among his own race at Namies. He could not visit the scherms of the other Hottentots; all were in the service of Trek-Boers, and the boycott against him was strict. As a protest against Max's unheard-of conduct in keeping such a man in his service, all the Boers had given strict injunctions to their servants to have nothing to do with the informer against Willem Bester. Besides, Gemsbok was; morally and intellectually, far in advance of all with whom he might, under other circumstances, have associated. Aristotle's aphorism as to the effect of solitude upon man is very true, and Gert Gemsbok had not become a beast in his exile.

Max noticed that now the old man never lost an opportunity of being near him. In the evenings, whenever Max happened to be in the shop, Gemsbok would come in, sit on the floor, and tell of his experiences. He thus told the true story of his life in detached fragments. And what a tale it was! what a lurid record of long-drawn, strenuous suffering made bearable, at first by the memory and afterwards by the companionship of a kindred mate! One night the old man told Max that he did not expect to live long; he felt his time had nearly come and he had no wish to prolong an existence which was now more than ever a weariness.

He did not, he said, care much whether he obtained any of the proceeds of the sale of the diamond or not; he had no desire now except to get enough food for himself and an occasional bite for his dog. The "Old Woman" was gone, and the sooner he too went the better.

His music now was all in a minor key; no more reels and jigs that made one long to caper. The old, stock melody ran through all he played, making it like an endless, barbaric fugue—weird and melancholy. His nocturnal performances sometimes made the dog leap out of the scherm and howl despairingly at the stars. In accompanying Oom Schulpad his hand seemed to have lost his cunning. The old fiddler would, however, sit for long periods, astonished and uncannily fascinated by the eerie tones scattered by the saddened strings of the ramkee.

Chapter Ten.

Nathan the Tempter.

One evening just after sunset Nathan arrived, driving a team of six smart mules before a brand-new cart. He had bought the turn-out at Clanwilliam on his return journey from Cape Town. He was accompanied by Koos Bester, at whose camp he had called in passing.

Nathan had entered into a contract to supply a firm of butchers in Cape Town with slaughter oxen; Bester, who owned a lot of cattle which were running, half-wild, in Bushmanland, agreed to sell him a certain number upon terms very advantageous to the purchaser.

Nathan was as unlike Max as it is possible for one brother to be unlike another. He was a low-sized, knock-kneed man of a fair complexion which burnt to a fiery red on the least exposure. His features were of the lowest Hebrew type—his lips were full and shapeless, his nose large and prominent, his eyes small and colourless, but exceedingly bright and glittering.

Since Max had awakened from boyhood to manhood he had come to hate this brother of his, to whom money was the only god worth worshipping, and who sneered at every impulse or aspiration that did not have gain for its object.

Next morning poor Max had a bad time of it. The books were examined, and when the debit entry against the Hattinghs came to light and Max was unable to give any satisfactory explanation as to why he had disregarded his instructions in allowing this account to be increased, Nathan treated him to the grossest abuse. However, things were found to be in a satisfactory condition on the whole; in fact Nathan could find nothing but this one item to find fault with. All day long he kept recurring to this one blot upon a good record, until at length Max became extremely angry and said that if Nathan would only stop talking about it he would pay the value of the articles sold out of his own salary. At this Nathan looked at him with a searching glint in his eye, but said nothing further on the subject.

In the afternoon Nathan went for a stroll among the camps, in the course of which he learned two things, namely, Max's relations with Susannah, and the fact that old Gert Gemsbok, the Hottentot, who had been placed under the ban for giving evidence against a Boer, was in his service. Nathan returned to the shop, filled with sardonic fury. Max at once saw that the hour he had been dreading for months had come.

"Well," said Nathan, after he had regarded his brother for a few seconds with an evil smile, "going to get married, eh?"

"Yes—what of that?" Max felt his courage rising; he no longer dreaded the thing before him.

"You, a Jew, and the child of Jews, to talk of marrying a Christian slut who was born under a bush and reared by stinking Boers in a mat-house?"

"If I am a Jew it is more than you are; you often said that you didn't believe in God."

"What has God got to do with it? A Jew is a Jew, God or no God, and a Christian is of no use except to make money out of. Nice idea, a chap like you thinking of getting married. Going to reside in this fashionable suburban villa, or do you mean to build a mansion for yourself?"

"Well, I sha'n't live here or anywhere else near you!"

Nathan blinked in astonishment; it was something quite unheard of, Max taking such a tone. The fear that inevitably strikes at the heart of the bully whenever even the weakest resists him, bridled his tongue for a minute; then he resumed—

"Well, you can take your Boer slut and breed babies under a koekerboom whenever you feel inclined, so far as I care; but if you want to stay on with me you will have to give up this rot."

"I do not want to stay another day with you," replied Max, in a quiet voice. "I want to have done with you as soon as I can, and then I shall not care if I never see you again."

Nathan, for the first time in his life, began to feel a glimmering of respect for his brother. However, it would not do to let Max see that this was the case. He began to expound upon the text of his other grievance—

"That old nigger you have hired; you must clear him out at once."

"You are master; if you want to get rid of him you had better give him notice. He is hired by the month."

"Yes, as soon as I can get another herd I will give your old pal notice with a sjambok. I'm not going to have my trade with the Boers spoilt by keeping on a damned old nigger-informer like that."

"I've got something belonging to him here," said Max, producing the diamond. "He picked it up on the bank of the river. He wants you to sell it and give him half the price."

Nathan took the stone and glanced at it. Then he gave a short whistle expressive of surprise and walked over to the window, in the light from which he examined the stone carefully. This done he slipped it into his trouser pocket and turned again to Max—

"No, my boy; that's a little too thin. Stones like this are not picked up in Bushmanland. This here diamond has been stolen from Kimberley, and I mean to keep it until I can restore it to its rightful owner. See?"

Here he winked. Max looked at him with deep scorn. Nathan left the shop and walked to a short distance, whistling a lively tune. Then he stood and critically regarded the sunset, with his hands in his pockets.

Soon afterwards old Gemsbok drove up the flock of sheep to where they always lay at night, on the side of the kopje behind the shop. Nathan called to him, and he came.

"Well, you're a nice sort of a scarecrow to come here spinning yarns about picking up diamonds in Bushmanland. I've a good mind to send you to the magistrate for having a stolen diamond in your possession."

"The diamond is not a stolen one, Baas."

"A likely story. I suppose you'll tell me next that you've never been to Kimberley, eh?"

"I have been to Kimberley, Baas."

"I thought so. Perhaps you'll tell me next that you've never been in the tronk, either, eh?"

"I have been in the tronk, Baas."

"Well, well; if that ain't wonderful guessing I'm a Dutchman. Beg your pardon, I'm sure"—here he grinned ironically at Max, who had just come out of the shop. "Let's try again. It might also be possible that your back has been tickled by the 'cat,' and that you didn't laugh, neither?"

"My back has felt the 'cat,' Baas."

"Ex-tra-ordinary! Why, I'm as good at pulling out facts as a corkscrew at opening bottles"—here he turned and winked at Max, who felt himself tingling with disgust. "Now look here, Mister Nigger-informer—who has been to the diamond fields, also in the tronk, to say nothing of other places, and whose back has been tickled by the 'cat' until you didn't laugh—I'm just going to stick to this here shining gem until I find the rightful owner. Of course, if you're not satisfied you can go and complain to the magistrate next time he comes round. See?"

"I see, Baas."

As Gert went to his scherm Nathan turned and winked to Max again. The latter walked away with rage and shame seething in him. Nathan went into the little back room and threw himself on the bed. He lay there and chuckled over the prize he had so easily acquired. "Why," he thought, "it must be worth at least fifty pounds." Well, at last his luck was properly booming. First, the big haul of feathers safely disposed of; next the cattle contract and the arrangement he had made with Koos Bester, under which Koos had to do all the work and he, Nathan, had only to pocket the profits; now this diamond. He began to calculate: at this rate he would be a rich man in a few years. Then he would go away and enjoy himself, would steep himself to the lips in vice, as he had often longed with the full strength of his weasel's soul to be able to afford to do.

A knock on the iron front of the door startled him from his dream.

"Come round here, whoever you are—especially if you have petticoats on!" he shouted.

Then the tread of a heavy man drew near, and Koos Bester entered the room.

"Well, Koos, my son, how do you feel this fine evening?"

"Fresh, thank you."

"Well, I don't know when I ever felt so happy. I don't know why I should" (here he thought he had been possibly injudicious in revealing his blissful condition to Koos) "after all the money I've been losing lately, and after the price I'm going to pay you for these cattle; but somehow I do."

Koos lit his pipe and smoked in silence. The Trek-Boer is seldom lively; in fact he is usually silent whenever he can possibly avoid speaking.

"Koos, have you heard that the old nigger who got Willem into that mess is here working for me, hired by my brother?"

"Ja, I heard so."

"Of course, I will give him the sack as soon as ever I can get another boy."

"Ja, I am glad to hear that."

"Koos, why don't you get him on the quiet and give him a good licking?"

"Ja, I should like to do that if you will not mind."

"Mind! No; I'll be only jolly glad if you will do it. But take him on the quiet, give him his dressing when there's no one about. Whatever you do, don't trust my brother; he makes quite a pal of him."

"Good, I'll make a plan. But when are we to start?"

"Let's see—this is Tuesday; supposing we get away on Friday. Say Friday morning at daylight."

"It'll be no use starting so early; we cannot get to my camp, round by Puffadder, in a day. It will be time enough to start after breakfast."

"But why do you want to go all that way round? Can't we go through the dunes?"

"No! you won't catch me going through the dunes this weather with mules. I have four horses that could do it; I wouldn't take them there now for five pounds."

"All right, Koos; we'll go round by Puffadder and start after breakfast on Friday."

The vast group of sand-dunes beyond which Koos Bester lived lies like a red-hot spider across the north-eastern section of the Desert, with the legs extending principally towards the south and south-west.

Rather, perhaps, is it like a menacing hand stretched forth by the giant Kalihari—that waterless waste of loose sand which extends northward indefinitely from just across the Orange River—to seize the southern extremity of the African Continent in a fiery grip. The river gorge cut the hand off at the wrist, else the eternal dribble might, in course of time, have overwhelmed all the western districts of the Cape Colony.

The dunes are, as a rule, only from ten to twenty feet in height, except in the central area where they are piled high about an abrupt, strange-looking hill which has a stratum of red stone encircling it like a belt. This hill is called "Bantom Berg," which means "belted mountain." The many mile-long fingers straggle over the Desert, gradually encroaching.

No one ever enters the dunes twice, except in case of the most urgent necessity. At every step the traveller sinks to below the ankles in the fine, light, scorching sand. It is sometimes practicable to cross the dune-tract in a light vehicle, if the weather happens to be cool and one's horses are in good condition. But crossing them is, however, never safe, for there is no water to be had within their repulsive bounds. The bones of many a lost wanderer lie there, covered by the sand streaming over the flat dune-top, under the lea of which he may have crept in the vain hope of getting shelter from the flame-hot wind from the north. In such a case the body would be buried deep, beyond the reach even of the jackals, in a very short time. If ever uncovered it would be found converted into a black, shrunken mummy, for the intense dryness of the sand is such that a body buried in it never decomposes; the moisture is rapidly drained out of it until nothing is left but a parchment bag of bones.

Max gave Nathan a month's notice of leaving next day. As, however, he had drawn his salary by the quarter, Nathan insisted on three months' notice being given. In this Max had to acquiesce, but he did so with a very bad grace.

Up to Friday morning Koos Bester had no opportunity of carrying out his intention of giving Gert Gemsbok a thrashing on the quiet. By Thursday night he had quite given up the idea. His slow mind had gradually come to recognise that he had better leave the old Hottentot alone—this in spite of Nathan's daily promptings on the subject. The old man looked so frail and bent. Some unrecognised remnant of chivalry in the Boer's nature made him dimly see that for a man of his strength to attack one who would be as a child in his hands would be base and cowardly. But Willem, whom he had loved as more than a brother, had been done to death by this baboon-like creature. Then for a few minutes the face of Koos would darken with the desire for revenge. He began to long for the time of departure, so as to be away from the temptation to do the deed that he loathed and longed for the doing of at the same time.

Friday morning came, and after breakfast Nathan and Koos departed from Namies in the cart drawn by the six smart mules. The road led around the kopjes to the westward, so the cart was out of sight of the camps a few minutes after the start.

The distance to Koos Bester's camp would take two short days to accomplish, but could not possibly be accomplished in one. The dunes were avoided on this route by passing over the point where the red-hot hand had been amputated and the stump frayed away by the winds of centuries. After travelling a mile or so they passed over some ground where a lot of shallow gullies, which carried off the occasional thunderstorm drainage from the kopjes, intersected each other. A flock of sheep could be seen grazing a few hundred yards to the right of the road, amongst the gullies. Between them and the road could be seen the figure of a man sitting on a doubled-down tussock of "twa" grass.

Koos felt the blood rise to his brain, but he averted his eyes from the figure and sucked violently at his pipe. Nathan pulled at the reins, and the mules came to a standstill. Just then the man arose from the tussock and disappeared over the edge of one of the gullies.

"Koos, my son, there's your chance."

"Never mind; I'll let the old vagabond alone to-day. I haven't got a sjambok with me, and that whip of yours wouldn't hurt him enough. Drive on."

"Rot! man alive; let's have some sport. Give him a taste of those pretty little feet of yours. Go on, I'll see fair play."

Koos alighted from the cart and began adjusting a part of the harness which had got out of gear. Then he walked back and put his foot on the step preparatory to climbing in.

"What! ain't you going to give it to him? Well, you most likely won't have another chance; I've told Max to give him the sack as soon as ever he can get another boy, so he'll likely be gone by the time we return."

Koos stood with his foot resting on the step, still undecided.

"Never mind," he said, "I'll let him alone to-day."

"And poor Willem, who died in the tronk all through that chap. Koos, I'm ashamed of you; be a man and give him what for."

Koos no longer hesitated. The reference to Willem turned the scale; his good angel soared away from his side for ever. The blood arose in his veins until his face and neck became purple. He uttered a curse and walked off, at first with hesitation still apparent in his movements. He was now eager to go, but his legs seemed reluctant to carry him. To harden his purpose he began to think of Willem's case; of how he had sworn to be revenged; of how a Boer, a man of his own blood, had been sent to herd with blacks at a convict station, and had there died miserably, all through the "thing" before him. At length his very bile seemed to stir with black rage, and he strode on with his hands and feet tingling for vengeance.

Gert Gemsbok watched over the edge of the gully the approach of Koos, and guessed the purpose of the Boer. Then he dropped back into the hollow behind him and ran down it as hard as he could in the hope of reaching some ground which he might tread on without leaving a spoor. He had caught up the little dog so that it should not betray him by following.

He might have escaped from Koos were it not that the cart stood on higher ground, and thus Nathan caught sight of his crouching form passing over an exposed spot. The Jew yelled to Koos that he was to trend to the left, and then indicated a small bush close to which he had caught sight of the fugitive. Koos, now thoroughly roused and thirsting madly for vengeance, started off at a run towards the bush Nathan had pointed out. In a few moments he nearly ran over the old Hottentot, who was hiding under an overhanging bank.

The sorry deed did not take long to accomplish. With his powerful hand Koos seized Gemsbok by the skinny arm and hurled him to the bottom of the gully. Not a word was spoken on either side. The old Hottentot was like a paper doll in the hands of the heavy, muscular Boer, and he fell with a thud upon the soft sand. Then Koos, beside himself with mad anger, leaped upon him like a tiger, stamped upon the shrunken body with his heavy feet, and kicked it until his toes, badly protected by the thin and supple-soled veldschoens, began to hurt him severely.

The pain brought Koos partly to himself. Casting one look upon the motionless, huddled body, he climbed out of the gully and began walking quickly back towards the cart. He found, however, that the great toe of his right foot caused him excruciating pain, so he could only limp slowly over the broken ground.

"Hello, Koos; did the old man show fight and knock you about? What's up with your little hind paw? Why, you look as white as a blooming sheet."

Koos climbed into the cart and Nathan drove on. There was something in the expression of the Boer's face which taught the Jew that it would not be safe to take any liberties just then.

After a few minutes Nathan found that he could sustain his curiosity no longer—

"Come along, old man," he said coaxingly; "tell us all about it."

Koos did not reply. He was in great pain, and was wondering what the effect of the particular kick which hurt him so had been on the man whom he kicked. His toe began to press against the upper-leather, and he felt that it was dislocated.

The still, huddled figure lying in the sand at the bottom of the gully was as if photographed on the retina—it was literally so vividly before his mental vision that physical vision seemed to be suspended. And the pain in his toe! He longed to take off the veldschoen and ease the pressure, to examine the injury, regarding which he was consumed with a deadly curiosity, but he hated to attract Nathan's attention.

He moved the foot slightly and the agony almost made him shriek aloud. A spasm of frantic terror gripped him by the heart-strings until he nearly swooned. Why, the man *must* be dead. He thought of his own bulk, of his strength, and of how passionately and recklessly he had leaped and stamped upon the nearly passive body. The details of what had happened had seemed lost to him for a time; in all but the merest and flimsiest general outline he had forgotten what had occurred between his gripping Gemsbok by the arm and his changing his walk into a hobble as he returned to the cart. Now, under some strange psychological sympathetic ink the smallest details appeared in pitiless distinctness, and stood out before his shuddering soul in lurid relief.

A wild rage against the man next to him, who had incited him to the deed—without whose fell, artful suggestion and encouragement his conscience would now have been clear—surged up in him. He felt, for a few minutes, as black an anger against Nathan as he had felt when he gripped the man he thought had wronged him, and dashed him down.

The day was hot and windless. He glanced up and saw the red-belted cone of Bantom Berg towering up amid the dunes. The cone was clear, and the waves of rarefied air quivered along the tops of the sand mounds like living flames, until they flashed into a lovely mirage away to the south, where the Desert line was unbroken.

He looked straight ahead and drew a deep sigh of relief, for red wisps of sand were tossing into the air, lashed by the fury of the first gusts of one of those fearful wind-storms from the north which were so common at that season. Soon the Desert would be tortured by moaning tempests, and then his footprints would be blotted out in the twinkling of an eye. A feeling of relief and subsequent elation swept through his mind. He was all right now; he had only been afraid of his spoor being found. He felt quite safe. They might, of course, suspect him; that did not matter, for Nathan, he knew, would never give information against him. Why, Nathan was almost an accomplice. The thought of his companion's knowledge of what he had done seemed to bring vague suggestions of disquiet in its trail; nevertheless his mind was able to poise itself still for a while on the dizzy pinnacle of elation to which it had swung out of the depths, impelled by a strange momentum. The Hottentot was dead—that was certain to him now. He seemed to be able to weigh and measure the force of every individual one of the kicks he had given, and the result of this sum in mental arithmetic was—death.

Nathan stole another glance at his companion's face and saw that it was now less terrible to look upon. His curiosity had become a positive pain. He felt he must venture to ask again for details.

"Come along, Koos," he coaxed; "tell us all about it."

"There's not much to tell. I just gave him a few thumps and left him."

"Why on earth didn't you bring him to the top of the bank and operate there? I didn't see any of the fun."

Here the Jew touched his companion's foot accidentally. Koos shrieked with anguish and uttered a horrible curse. Nathan seemed very much astonished. He riveted his gaze on the foot.

"Why, Koos, there's blood on your veldschoen. Did you cut your foot?"

Koos could stand the pain no longer. He lifted his foot upon his left knee and began to untie the reimpje with which the veldschoen was tied. Nathan stopped the mules.

When the veldschoen was removed the great toe was found to be dislocated. It had turned from its usual direction and was pointing backward, owing to the strain on the tendon. The whole front part of the foot was turning purple.

"My eye!" said Nathan, "you must have given it to him precious hot. Why, you've unlatched your blooming big toe. That ain't your blood, neither. My eye! And I didn't see it happening. Just like my luck!"

Koos felt sick with pain. He wrapped his jacket around the injured foot and leant back. The sand-storm swept down in fury. Nathan relieved his feelings by fluent cursings. To Koos the fiery wind with its burthen of stinging sand was more grateful than the zephyrs of a springtime dawn.

"Ain't it lucky we didn't take the road through the dunes?" shouted Nathan during a slight comparative cessation of the wind.

Koos did not reply. He was wishing with the full strength of his tortured soul that they had taken the dune route, whatever its dangers might have been, in preference to the one which had led him to the scene of his crime.

They reached the water-place which is known by the name of "Puffadder," and there saw the mat-houses of several Trek-Boer camps. By agreement it was stated that Koos had injured his foot by hitting it, when running, against a stone. An old woman who was skilled in herbal remedies and rough surgery made him lie down on his back upon the ground. Then she tied a thin reim around the dislocated toe and got two of her sons to haul at it. The toe slipped back into its socket, but Koos fainted from the pain. When he came to himself the evil face of Nathan was peering into his. He closed his eyes to shut out the sight of that which he had now come to hate as he had never hated anything before.

"Well, old man," said Nathan, "it strikes me you must have smashed that blooming stone you ran your foot against into splinters."

After the mules had been watered and had taken a roll in the sand another start was made. The old woman had boiled down some dried herbs in a tin pannikin and tied rags soaked in the decoction around the injured toe. This treatment relieved the pain considerably. When they inspanned and made another start the wind had completely ceased, the sunlight had lost its sting, and the stillness of infinite peace seemed to brood like a bright-plumaged dove over the Desert. There was no sound but the faint creak-creak of the harness as the mules trotted along over the soft sand. Nathan made several attempts to elicit further particulars as to what Koos had done to the old Hottentot, but his companion remained obstinately silent, and he felt instinctively that it would not be safe for him to pursue the subject farther just then.

The sun was nearly down when they reached Koos Bester's camp on the following day. In the interval the mind of the unhappy Boer had perpetually oscillated between two poles—that of remorse, terror, and despair on the one hand, and that of unreasoning elation on the other. But he would not speak of the thing which had happened. Sometimes he persuaded himself that the old Hottentot was surely dead; anon he reasoned that the proverbial physical toughness of the race to which the man belonged would enable him to recover. But the limp, passive, huddled form, prone on the sand at the bottom of the gully, haunted him with deadly persistence, and his detestation of the Jew who had persuaded him against his will to do the deed grew in intensity.

The collecting of the cattle, which ranged over a couple of thousand square miles of Desert, occupied several days. Nathan made himself as agreeable as possible to Mrs Bester and the children, who, however, cordially and instinctively disliked him. Koos turned upon him from time to time a slow gaze in which smouldering hatred seemed to lurk. This was especially noticeable when the Jew, as he often did, began paying Mrs Bester extravagant compliments.

Koos' foot became much better under the treatment recommended by the old woman who had assisted him at Puffadder. She had given him a supply of her medicinal herbs, and of these infusions were made, the application of which was followed by the best results.

Koos had repeated to his wife and her father the story as to his having injured his foot by hitting it against a stone. The father-in-law caused some embarrassment by questioning him closely as to the details of the accident. The answers were not very consistently given, and when the discrepancies were commented on Koos lost his temper. Nathan was present at this scene and keenly enjoyed it.

After the cattle had been collected and the number purchased by Nathan selected and marked, the latter took his departure. In returning to Namies he followed the course he had come by. When nearly home he glanced regretfully in the direction of the broken gullies, thinking of the piece of sport he had missed, on the details of which Koos Bester had been so strangely reticent.

Next morning Koos inspanned his cart just after daybreak. He could no longer endure the suspense of waiting for information as to the result of his violence. He drove a team of rough ponies, the equals of which for endurance could hardly have been found in Bushmanland. He travelled in a light cart which had no hood. As the day seemed to promise coolness he decided to venture on taking the road through the dunes.

Chapter Eleven.

The Broken Ramkee.

About half an hour after the departure of Nathan and Koos Bester from Namies Max was surprised to see Gert Gemsbok's dog running back from the veld with every appearance of terror. It rushed straight to the scherm, and there stood panting and with air erect along its back. Its ears were cocked and its tail tucked under, as it gazed back in the direction whence it came, sniffing the time with wide, dilated nostrils. This struck Max as extremely strange and eerie. He knew the habits of this dog; never since Gemsbok had rescued it had the animal left the side of its master.

Oom Schulpad happened to come to the shop shortly afterwards, and Max mentioned the circumstance to him. Together they walked up the side of the kopje to the scherm. The dog was so preoccupied by whatever was the cause of its agitation that it appeared unaware of their approach until they got quite close to it. Then the animal crept in under the fence of bushes and lay there whining.

"That dog has had a fright," said Oom Schulpad. "I have sometimes seen dogs like that, and it was always after they had seen something bad happen. See, now, if something has not happened to the old Bushman."

Max returned to the shop. After dinner, as no customers were about, he started out to search for Gert Gemsbok. He went up to the scherm and caught the dog. At first the animal snapped and snarled when he approached it. Max had, however, taken some pieces of meat with him, and these he held out in propitiation. Thus mollified, the dog allowed itself to be caught and a reim tied around its neck.

The Desert was a whirling hell of blinding and scorching sand-clouds. Max staggered on along the course which he had seen Gemsbok take that morning with his flock. The dog at first showed the most violent disinclination to follow, and had to be dragged along struggling and biting at the reim.

During a lull in the wind Max saw that the sheep were scattered about in groups far distant from each other; some were sheltering themselves among the stones on the side of the kopje and others were far out on the plain. He took his course towards the farthest group of sheep that he could distinguish. The dog now became very much excited; every now and then it would tug at the reim and try to bound forward in a certain direction. Then it would recoil in terror and endeavour to bolt back.

Max worked his way onward across the gullies in the direction indicated by the dog's alarmed gaze. At length he reached the edge of a gully, on the opposite side of which was an overhanging bank. Huddled under this, as though to get shelter from the wind, he recognised the motionless form of Gert Gemsbok.

Lying about in the sand, and partly covered by its drift, was the ramkee, shattered into fragments. Gemsbok was lying half on his face, with his head leaning forward on his arm. Max bent over, and as soon as he ascertained that his old friend was faintly breathing, spoke his name. Gemsbok tried to lift his head, but failed in the attempt. Then Max gently passed his arm around the bruised body, and drew it back until the head rested on his shoulder.

The poor old man opened his eyes. They were dull and glazed. Then he moaned heavily and went off into a faint. Max noticed that the head was swollen on one side, and that a small trickle of blood came from the mouth. The wind had almost ceased, so Max drew Gert's limp body tenderly down the loose sandbank and laid him on his back. After a few seconds he returned to consciousness, and the eyelids again lifted—very slowly this time.

In a broken gasp he uttered the word "Water!"

Max sprang up, meaning to run back to Namies and fetch a drink, but Gemsbok motioned to him to come close. Max bent over him again.

"Baas Max... leave... the water... it is... too late... I die for... the old sin... In my bag... sewn up... there is something... They are yours... I came honestly... by them..."

Then the head fell back, and with a low moan of pain Gert Gemsbok drew his last breath—an obscure martyr in the cause of Truth, at whose deserted shrine in the Desert he had worshipped to his own despite.

Max tried to revive him, but soon found that his attempts were useless. The dog sat on the bank at the edge of the gully, giving vent to long-drawn howls.

Max stood and looked at the body through a mist of blinding tears. Then he gathered up the fragments of the instrument which had been the only solace of the man lying dead before him through years of misery, and laid them reverently at the side of the corpse. He closed the lids of the dim and tired eyes and tied up the fallen jaw with his pocket-handkerchief. In doing this his hand came in contact with the reim by which the skin bag was slung over the dead man's shoulder. This reminded him of the words with which Gemsbok had gasped out his life. He drew the bag softly away and began to examine its contents.

He found a pipe, a tinder box, tobacco, some dried roots, and a few strings for the ramkee in course of preparation out of sinew; nothing else. Then he discovered that the bottom of the bag had been sewn up from corner to corner, and that some hard bodies were secured under the sewn portion. He ripped open the stitches and the five diamonds rolled into his hand.

Max gazed in astonishment at the stones for a few seconds and then slipped them into his pocket. He felt dazed by all he had experienced. He sat down to collect his scattered thoughts. He looked once more upon the dead face. The diamonds were at once forgotten, and he burst into passionate sobs. The weight of all the wickedness of the world seemed to press upon him, and a sense of the futility of good darkened his soul.

He climbed out of the gully and hastened back to Namies. In a few moments all the men there were on their way to the spot where Gert Gemsbok lay as if enjoying a peace in death such as he had never known when living.

It was Old Schalk's duty as Assistant Field Cornet to hold an inquest, and, if there were discovered the slightest sign of foul play, to send immediately a report on the subject to the magistrate.

The body was stripped, and was found to be horribly bruised and swollen. The Assistant Field Cornet at once gave it as his opinion that the deceased had come to his death through being thrown from a horse.

"It is well known," said he, "that these Bushmen are in the habit of catching the Boers' horses in the veld and riding their tails off."

"But," broke in Max, "this man never interfered with anybody's—"

"Young man," said Old Schalk with severity, "when you have lived as long in Bushmanland, and seen as many dead Bushmen as I have seen, you'll perhaps be entitled to give an opinion."

"But," said Max excitedly, "the man told me just before he died that—"

"Young man," interrupted Old Schalk, who had made a shrewd guess as to the perpetrator of the deed, and felt that his duty to the Trek-Boers of Bushmanland forbade him to permit indiscreet revelations, "are you the Field Cornet or am I? What does it matter what he told you—who ever knew a Bushman tell the truth? It is well known that Oom Dantje van Rooyen has a very vicious horse, which only last year threw a man to the ground and then kicked and bit him. That very horse is running in this veld at present—I saw it myself only yesterday. I am quite sure that nothing but the horse did this. The case is quite clear."

A buzz of approval on the part of the Boers followed this verdict. Here was a dead Bushman whose body showed lesions and appearances such as might be caused by equestrian misadventure. Grazing somewhere in the neighbourhood was a horse which had been known to kick and bite a man after it had thrown him. Of course the case was perfectly clear.

Max looked around the ring of faces and saw nothing but amusement at his warmth of expression, mingled with slyness, depicted upon them. There was no pity for the sufferings which the man must have endured before he died—no horror that such a deed had been perpetrated by one with whom they were on terms of intimacy upon a sentient human being, was suggested. He felt an arm slipped within his. Looking round he saw the inscrutable visage of Oom Schulpad close beside him.

"Come, children, let us go and drink some coffee," said Old Schalk as he led the way, assisted by a stalwart Boer, to the cart which had conveyed him from his camp to the nearest available point.

As the others followed in small groups Oom Schulpad heard one young Boer say to another—

"Got, kerel, maar Koos hat die ou' Boschmann lekker geskop."

(God, old fellow, but Koos kicked the old Bushman nicely.)

Oom Schulpad gave a sardonic grin which might have been expressive of anything, from rapture to nausea, and turned back to where Max was sitting fuming with indignation and grief. He laid a sympathetic hand upon the boy's shoulder and bent his rough face, which now bore a kindly expression, over him.

"Never mind, child," he said, "the poor old schepsel is not going to suffer any more pain. Who knows but he may be with the old woman now, and she, perhaps, may have got a new pair of legs."

"But the man has been murdered," replied Max hotly, "and he wants to screen the murderer—"

"Shush, shush. Young tongues gallop into dangerous places. What good can you do by making a disturbance? You won't bring the old Bushman to life again, and it would be a bad thing for him if you could. Besides, a man must never try to set the world right all by himself."

"But he wouldn't hear what I had to say. I shall let the Government know what sort of a Field Cornet he is."

"And get nothing for your pains except the hatred of every one about here. What does the Government care? It only wants not to be troubled about things. When you are as old as I am you will not be put out by anything done by people like Old Schalk."

"I shall send a letter off at once to the magistrate and ask him to come here and see for himself."

"No, I think you had better do nothing of the kind. If you did, the magistrate and the doctor would perhaps arrive in three weeks from now and when they came what would they be able to find out from the body? Besides, in that case it would probably turn out that some one had seen him riding Oom Dantje's horse, or had even seen him thrown and trampled on. No, you had better do nothing at all but just bury the old Bushman. I liked him because he knew more music than I did. Come, I will help you to bury him. We'll dig his grave next to where the old woman lies—among the kopjes. I'll inspan my donkeys and we'll draw him up in the cart."

Max and Oom Schulpad wended back to Namies, and, with a couple of spades which they took out of the shop, soon dug a grave in the sluit at the back of the little kopje. It was easy ground to work, and, in spite of his deformity, Oom Schulpad was a first-rate hand at digging. In a little more than half an hour the grave was ready, and then Oom

Schulpad harnessed his donkeys to the little cart and drove down to fetch the body.

Max had brought some clean, white linen from the shop, and in this they wrapped the earthly remains of Gert Gemsbok, the lonely, martyred votary at Truth's neglected shrine. The fragments of the ramkee were reverently tied together by the old fiddler, who was honest artist enough to acknowledge a superior when he met him. He laid the shattered instrument where the stiffened hand might press upon the slackened strings until both turned to dust.

The full moon lifted her sweet face over the rim of the world, and, under the spell of her smile, the Desert took on beauty of a weird and unearthly kind. The plumy heads of the grass became pendant with dew-diamonds; every tussock was transformed into a fairy-forest lit by sparkling lamps. The ice-plants glinted so brightly that they seemed to merge together a few yards from the observer's feet, and from there to form a shining pathway to the moon.

The strange funeral *cortège* wended up between the camps of Namies. Oom Schulpad walked at the side, holding the reins; Max, with bent head, followed close behind the body.

So they laid Gert Gemsbok in the sand, next to his "Old Woman" and with his broken ramkee at his side. If what some tell us about a future life be true, that ramkee will surely be recreated in the celestial equivalents of the rarest earthly instruments of music—if not something as valuable and more sonorous.

Old Schalk was sitting in the moonlight at the door of his mat-house talking to a few cronies when the funeral passed. A silence fell upon all when they saw what it was that the patient donkeys were hauling up the hill through the heavy sand. Just after the vehicle had passed out of sight around the flank of one of the kopjes Old Schalk broke the silence. He turned to one of his companions and said—"I never yet knew a man who could play the fiddle well who was not a little mad."

Chapter Twelve.

The Bondage of Koos Bester.

Max's mourning for his old friend was deep and sincere. The heart of the young man, from its first awakening, recoiled from the sordidness of most of those with whom he had come in daily contact, and clave to the best within its reach—this by virtue of its natural intuitions. For a time it seemed as though a blank had been created which could never be filled. The evenings spent in the shop when Oom Schulpad and Gemsbok had contended like a couple of troubadours—the weird tales of his experiences during the six years of his banishment from the tents of men, which the old waif had related with such tragic and truthful pathos—his devotion to his miserable old wife, that decayed relic of womanhood, which was as tender as ever his love could have been for the companion of his early years—all these dwelt in the mind of Max and tinged it with what he deemed would be an abiding sadness.

On the other hand the acquisition of the five diamonds had materially improved his prospects. He hid them in a safe place and determined not to mention the fact of their existence to any one but Susannah. They were stones of very pure water, averaging about ten carats each in weight. Max knew that they must be very valuable, but he was unable to guess their worth. He made up his mind that he would have to take them to Europe and realise them there.

Even Oom Schulpad seemed to be depressed by the old Hottentot's fate. When he now came to see Max of an evening he did not bring his violin. The two would just sit and smoke in silence, each well aware of what was filling the thoughts of the other. To Max it seemed as if the ghost of the slain man haunted the room on these occasions, asking why his only friends had not taken vengeance upon his slayer.

Oom Schulpad did not believe very much in anything outside the circle of his experiences—certainly not in ghosts. He had attained to a philosophy which might be summed up in a phrase—"Never interfere in anything that does not directly concern you." His stock formula into which the foregoing principle had crystallised was—"No man should ever rub resin on any but his own bow."

"But," he continued one night after reiterating this phrase several times, "I mean to scratch Koos Bester's nose with a certain piece of resin which I have in my pocket. He had no business to put his big hands upon any man who could make music like that, Bushman or no Bushman."

Max pricked up his ears and looked at the old fiddler with a question in his eyes.

"I know Koos," continued Oom Schulpad, "and if he does not bark his shins as well as his nose against the lump of resin which I will put in his path—well, I'm no fiddler and the Bushman knew no music. He said my back was like a springbuck's when it 'pronks,' did he, and that my mouth was as poisonous as a sand-adder's? Also he broke the ramkee—to say nothing of killing the old Bushman."

"What do you intend to do to him?" queried Max.

"I'll tell you that when he comes back, my child. It will be all right, don't fear. You shall, perhaps, help me. I know Koos well. When he was quite a big boy he used to be afraid of being alone in the dark. I'll make him dance a new step to the old Bushman's music. Ja, he knew more music than I, that old Bushman."

Three days elapsed after the tragedy before Max visited the Hattingh camp. He found Old Schalk looking extremely sulky. Max, however, had ceased to take much heed of people or their moods. He no longer dreaded Old Schalk. As in the case of Mrs Hattingh, he now felt he had him at a moral disadvantage. His recent experiences had tended to give Max considerable self-confidence.

He found Susannah alone in the mat-house, and asked her to go with him for a walk. As they passed out it seemed as though the old man sitting in the chair meant to stop them. He bent forward with an angry expression, removed the pipe from his mouth, and opened his lips as if to speak. Max, however, looked him steadily in the face, so he remembered his account at the shop—it seemed as though Nathan meant to stay away indefinitely—and Old Schalk's sack of coffee was running very low indeed. At the same instant he thought of the inquest—the menace which he seemed to read in Max's face might perhaps have reference to that judicial triumph. Whilst these considerations were working through his mind the lovers passed him and he made no protest. They climbed the big kopje and again sat at the foot of the large koekerboom.

Max poured out his sorrow and indignation in a flood. Susannah had been told simply that Gert Gemsbok had met his death through an accident in connection with a horse. She had seen the strange funeral and wondered thereat. Now Max's account of the old Hottentot's life, which she had never heard before, and of his cruel and mysterious death, moved the girl to deep sympathy.

A horrible suspicion had haunted Max from the first—he could not avoid connecting his brother with the murder, for such he was convinced had occurred. Nathan had taken his departure with Koos Bester just before the deed was done; it was inconceivable that he could be ignorant of the crime. Max believed him to be fully capable of participating in the commission of any evil.

When Susannah questioned him as to whom he suspected, Max tried hard to avoid replying. When he could no longer do this he told the girl all his thoughts and then bent his head on her knee and wept bitter tears. It was the shame of being related to a creature such as Nathan which struck him to the heart. A hatred of his surroundings, and more especially of his brother, had been born in him. He made up his mind to leave his brother's service at once, come what might.

"Susannah, I can stay here no longer; will you come away with me?"

The girl did not reply. She sat thinking of what the consequences of such a step would be. Her utter inexperience of life was strongly qualified by natural caution, as well as by that instinct of self-preservation which clothes most women like an armour of proof.

"I feel I can stay here no longer," he continued. "Leaving out Oom Schulpad and yourself, I hate and despise every one here. Will you come away with me?"

"I will go with you when you marry me, Max."

"How can I marry you when you are only nineteen and your uncle will not give his consent?"

"I will wait for you. Go away, and you will find me here when you come back—if there is any water left in the well."

"I do not want to go away without you, and I feel I cannot endure to stay. Why are you afraid to trust me?"

"I am not afraid to trust you, but—while you were talking at first I was thinking. I thought to myself that we could not get away and that there was no place for us to go to."

"You can leave all that to me—"

"No, no, it cannot be. If you want to marry me, Max, you must make up your mind never to live in any place but Bushmanland—"

"What! live all our lives at Namies?"

"No, not at Namies. Bushmanland is large; there are many camps and many water-places in it. You know that I am only a poor Boer girl and that I could not live among those women whose pictures you showed me in the fashion books and who never speak anything but English; you would be ashamed of me and I should want to come back to live among the people I know."

Max, after the manner of lovers, assured her that he never could, under any possible circumstances, be ashamed of her. She continued in the same strain as formerly—

"I once saw some girls who went past our camp in a wagon, when we dwelt on the other side of the Desert, far away to the eastward, and I felt like a Bushwoman beside them when I noticed their clothes and heard them talk. No, Max, I will never go to any place where you would be able to compare me with women such as those."

Max assured her that she could easily challenge comparison with any girl in South Africa for physical advantages. Her colour heightened with pleasure at his compliments, but she was not to be moved from her resolution.

"Max, I shall never live in any place outside Bushmanland, so you had better make up your mind to that. Besides, you will have to wait for me until I am old enough to marry without my uncle's consent. Bushmanland is long and wide, but when a girl is talked about for doing what you want me to do, the tongues of the women are heard, louder than thunder, from one side of it to the other. If I were to do this thing the people of the only land I can live in would look upon me as being no better than a Hottentot girl at the Copper Mines."

Max felt, instinctively, that the girl was right. He made no further attempt to move her, but he reconsidered his decision about leaving Namies at once. At all events he would wait for Nathan's return. As the lovers walked back to the camp, they said few words to each other.

Nathan returned late in the afternoon of the next day. The brothers met outside the shop. Nathan greeted Max with cheerfulness, as though he wished to ignore what had last passed between them. Max looked him straight in the eyes without acknowledging his salute.

"Hello," said Nathan, "got the hump, eh?"

Max went into the shop; Nathan followed him after outspanning the horses. In the meantime the flock of sheep had been driven home by a strange herd. Nathan burned with curiosity to know what had transpired. He walked up to Max and addressed him again—

"Where's your old chum? I see you've got a new nigger."

Max gave him a contemptuous glance and then went on with what he had been doing, without replying to the question.

"Are you deaf?"

"I'm not deaf; neither am I blind."

"Then why the devil don't you answer me? Where's the old nigger?"

"Mightn't he be lying dead in a sluit where you and Koos Bester left him last week?"

"Look here, none of your blasted conundrums. I didn't pull you out of a Whitechapel gutter and bring you here to get lip from you."

Max went on with his occupation of tidying the goods upon the shelves, without making any reply. Nathan, furious, strode round the counter and gripped him by the arm. Max turned and gazed steadily into his eyes.

"You bastard Christian dog, if you don't answer my question I'll make pork sausages of you!"

Max seized Nathan by the throat and flung him backwards. The latter's foot caught against the corner of a box and he fell sprawling under the counter. As he picked himself up Max strode towards him. Nathan recoiled in alarm; he had not expected such treatment from the shy, silent, diffident lad whom he had been in the habit of cuffing and cursing at whenever he felt in a bad temper and wanted to relieve his feelings.

"Where is he?" shouted Max in a voice strident with rage. "He is where you will never be—in an honest man's grave. He lived long enough to let me know that you and Koos Bester are murderers. I only regret that he did not let me know enough to hang you both."

Nathan quailed; he wondered how much Gemsbok had told. Then he cast up the column of possibilities in his mind. No, he was all right. There might be suspicion, but there could be no proof that he had been accessory to the crime. However, it would be just as well not to provoke Max any further at present. He walked out of the shop and Max closed the door behind him.

The Desert twilight was quickly fading. Nathan wished to be alone, so he strolled past the camps without calling at any of them, and then back along the road he had just previously travelled.

After he had passed the last camp by about a hundred yards he sat down on a stone. He was sunk in the deepest thought. An idea had struck him just after Max's outburst and had taken root, branched and burgeoned until it seemed to be a tree full of flowers which promised rich fruit. The muffled thud of tired horses' feet on the sandy road leading from the dunes broke in upon his reverie. He lifted his head from where it had been sunk upon his breast and chuckled with unclean mirth.

"Well, I think I'm in jam *this* time," soliloquised he; "whole blooming coppers of it."

When he returned home Max was not on the premises. The shop was locked, but the little room at the back where Nathan slept was open. Of late Max had taken to sleeping on the counter in the shop.

Nathan lit a candle and began to undress. The elation of his mind was evinced upon his face. He went to bed and softly whistled the tune of a music-hall song as he lay back on the pillow with his hands clasped at the back of his head. He felt extremely happy. His luck was in—this last development, over which he had been chuckling so, proved that conclusively.

Again the sound which he had heard when sitting on the stone broke in on his waking dreams, the slow tramp, tramp, tramp of the feet of tired horses, muffled by the soft sand. This time the sound came from much nearer than before. Then he heard the creaking of the vehicle and the wisch-wisch of the ploughing wheels. Then the sound ceased. A few moments later he heard a stealthy step approaching the door; just afterwards came a light tap.

"Who is there?" he called out.

"Open the door quickly. It is I, Koos."

Nathan sprang out of bed and drew back the bolt. Koos at once stepped into the room and glanced furtively around. His face looked drawn and haggard and his eyes were bloodshot.

"Are you alone?" he asked, in a husky voice.

"Yes, I am alone. But be careful, I don't know where Max is."

Koos bent forward until his dry lips almost touched Nathan's ear, and whispered—

"What has happened? Tell me quickly."

Nathan drew back slightly and let the ghost of a mocking smile flit over his features.

"Oh, I got home all right, thanks. But what brings you here?"

The Boer leant forward across the table and grasped the Jew's wizened shoulder in his enormous hand. Nathan shuddered convulsively under the pressure; he thought his bones were being crushed. The eyes of Koos seemed to shoot forth dusky flames.

"Tell me quickly," he said.

"All right," said Nathan, trying hard to wrench himself free, and feeling, at the same time, that it might be dangerous to take liberties with the man before him, "I'll tell you, unless you break my blooming back first of all. You kicked a little too hard, Koos; the old nigger is dead."

The visage of Koos became frightful. He gasped for breath and a low gurgle came from his throat. He sat silent for a few moments with his eyes fixed upon Nathan's in a burning stare. Then he said in a strained, hoarse voice—

"Tell me more. Tell me all about it."

"That's all I know about it myself."

Koos arose slowly from his seat and stretched his hands out towards Nathan, who, seeing murder in his eye, retreated into the corner.

"Stop, Koos!" he almost screamed. "So help me God, I know nothing more about it than what I've told you. I only came home just before you did."

Koos sank back into the chair and covered his face with his hands. After a few minutes he arose and staggered out of the room. He went to where his tired horses were still standing in the harness, outspanned them, and after tying the front legs of each together with a reim, turned them out to graze. Then he wrapped himself in his kaross, for the night air was chilly, and laid himself down under the cart.

He could not sleep. It seemed to him as if he had never slept, as if the axis upon which the hollow globe of stars turned was laid through his brain, as if there were no such thing as sleep in the whole wide world. The sky was clear and limpid, as only the sky which leans over and seems to love the Desert can be. The sweet, piercing smell of the dew-wet sand came to him and brought memories of nights spent on the hunting-field, when the pungent scent, the very breath and essence of the quick earth, had seemed to renew his spent strength, after the fatigues of the chase. But then he had not stained his hands with blood.

But the awful silence. Would nothing break it? It seemed to press upon and crush him like something ponderable and tangible. He lifted his fist and smote lightly the bottom of the cart just over his head. The sound seemed to split his brain like an axe. Then the returning wave of silence surged around him, and under its impact he seemed to sink as into a quicksand.

At length, a sound. Far away on the waste he heard the long-drawn nasal, melancholy howl of a jackal. Before the weird cry came to an end it was taken up by others at a greater distance, and then repeated on and on like the challenges of crowing cocks in the dawning.

A gush of gratitude came from his darkened heart; he felt that he almost loved the prowling brutes that had drawn his soul out of the quagmire of silence in which it had been sunk. He seemed to feel a kind of fellowship and sympathy with the jackals. He wondered why this was. Then he remembered—

The waning moon had been making paler the western stars, but he had not noticed it. The straining of his sound-sense had left no room for that of sight to come into play. Now the spell of silence was broken, and the sense of sight began to assert itself.

His eyes had been closed for some little time. When he opened them the Desert was flooded with a gentle haze of diaphanous pearl. This made the Namies kopjes look like a group of enchanted islands floating in an unearthly sea. The scene was almost too beautiful for mortal eyes.

As the moon soared higher and higher the stones and bushes, which at a few paces' distance could not be separated from their shortening shadows, took on strange and ever-changing shapes. God! What was that a few yards from him? Surely they cannot have brought the body up from the gully and left it exposed upon the kopje-side? Yes, there it lay, huddled and horrible.

He must go and look at it—examine it—even if the doing of this killed him or drove him mad. He arose to a crouching position and passed slowly across the intervening space of a few yards with hesitating steps. He bent his horror-distorted face over a stone half hid in tufted pelargonium.

Day came near. The glamour and mystery receded from the Desert, gathered into a wave and broke against the splendid gates of dawn. A short and troubled sleep fell upon the wretched man under the cart, and perhaps saved him for the time being from insanity. He awoke to find the flaming sun high in the brazen sky, and the camp at his feet astir with life.

In the full light of day Koos Bester could hardly realise that he had been a prey to the horrors of the damned during the long hours of the previous night. His terrors had vanished with the distorting moonlight. What did it matter, after all? It was true that Nathan could put the rope around his neck with a word, but he easily persuaded himself the word would never be spoken. His conscience was still sore, but not agonisingly so, now in the daylight. A Bushman was, after all, only a Bushman, and the mind of the Boer always draws an important distinction between a "mens" and a "schepsel."

He felt hungry, so he strolled down through the camps on the lookout for a breakfast. He did not want to eat with Nathan again if he could possibly avoid doing so. He knew that he must expect to have to run the gauntlet of covert allusion and innuendo. He knew that suspicion of having done the deed—the memory of which hung around his neck like a millstone—had already marked him, in the estimation of some, at least, as a sort of minor Cain. This, however, he was prepared for, and he could meet the prospect with calmness. He was now high at the dizzy extreme of hopeful confidence, resting for the instant's pause before the return swing of the pendulum to which he was bound, like Ixion to the wheel, should whirl him back towards the ledges of anguish where the vultures of remorse were perched, waiting to tear anew at his vitals.

He was consumed by an apprehensive curiosity which burnt him like a fever. He longed to hear all about the finding of the body, or—horrible thought!—had the man been still alive when found? No, that was impossible; his reason told him from the heights of reassurance, had such been the case he would have been apprehended long before this.

As he walked furtively along, still limping slightly from the effects of the dislocated toe, he glanced hurriedly from side to side from under his bent brows. He fancied he was being watched from every mat-house. Yes, he was. In the gloom of every doorway he could see the dim faces of women and children turned in his direction. Even thus, he imagined, must the Lord have set a mark upon Cain, that all mankind might know him. It seemed as though by some subtle means every one throughout the scattered camps had simultaneously become aware of his presence. Just before descending the hill from where his cart stood outspanned he had heard laughter and the shrill voices of children at play. Now all was mute in an awful, accusing hush. The sudden silence reminded him of what he had suffered during the night, before the jackals claimed fellowship with him, and passed the word of his initiation into their brotherhood across the listening Desert. He felt that the brand of Cain, which none may describe but which none may fail to recognise, was upon him.

Old Schalk was sitting before his tent, smoking. Koos made an effort, and, turning abruptly in his course, walked up and greeted him. Old Schalk returned the salutation with more than ordinary friendliness, and then offered a chair and the inevitable cup of coffee. These were gratefully accepted. The old Boer called to Susannah to bring the coffee. She was in the wagon and was thus unaware of the identity of the visitor. When she came from the scherm with the cup she coloured angrily and her eye flashed. She passed the visitor the cup, but did not offer her hand in greeting. Koos winced. Among the Boers such an omission can only be construed as a deliberate insult.

Old Schalk was in great form. From the first glance at the face of his visitor he knew beyond the shadow of a doubt that the slayer of Gert Gemsbok was before him. His previous suspicions were so strong that little room for any doubt had existed in his mind. Here, however, was proof, writ large for all to read. Old Schalk was extremely tolerant where the killing of Bushmen was concerned, and it distressed him genuinely to see Koos take a comparative trifle so much to heart. Old Schalk fell into the error of ascribing *all* of Koos' distress to mere fright, so he determined to try and put him at his ease. Koos had been watched carefully since his arrival, and Old Schalk knew it was probable that he was seeking information as to what had transpired since the commission of the deed.

"Did you hear of the accident the other day?" the old man asked, without looking at the man he addressed.

"Ja—that is—I heard something—"

"I have often said that an accident would come from letting that horse of Oom Dantje's run where he can be caught and ridden by the Bushmen."

"What did Oom Dantje's horse do?" said Koos, breathlessly.

Old Schalk shot a glance at him out of the corner of one eye, and looked puzzled. It was evident that Koos had not even heard of the verdict.

"Well, no one saw the horse do it, you know; but from the way that old Bushman was knocked about, I think—myself—that it must have been Oom Dantje's horse. I reported so to the magistrate."

Koos set down the empty utensils upon the ground. The cup rattled like castanets upon the saucer. A sense of blissful peace seemed to descend upon him like a dove with healing wings. It was the revulsion of feeling which made him tremble.

"Yes," continued old Schalk, "that young Jew, Max, wanted to talk some nonsense about what the old Bushman had told him before he died, but I wouldn't listen. It's all right, Koos—you needn't look like that."

The dove had changed, in the twinkling of an eye, into a vulture; its beak was imbedded in his heart-strings. This was the contingency he had dismissed as being impossible—the man's having been found alive. He must find out what the dying Hottentot had said, or else go mad. He arose, shook hurriedly the moist hand of his host with his own burning one, and then limped painfully back towards the shop.

Oom Schulpad had watched Koos carefully ever since he arose from his feverish sleep under the cart. The old fiddler was staying, just then, with some people who had camped on the site formerly occupied by Koos; he was sitting in the mat-house with his fiddle on his knee, when Koos came limping up the sandy slope. Then the tones of the air which Gemsbok so often had played upon the ramkee were slowly wailed out from the strings in a minor key. Koos stiffened as though he had received an electric shock, and stood stock still for an instant. Then he resumed his limping towards the shop.

Both Nathan and Max were in the iron building; the former writing at the empty packing-case which served as a desk, and the latter engaged in bartering wild-cat skins from some strange Hottentots from Great Namaqualand. One of the strangers carried a ramkee slung upon his back. This was not a very unusual circumstance, but to Koos it was an item full of horrible significance.

The barter was soon over. Max leaped across the counter and passed out through the door, cutting Koos dead. Nathan came forward, greeted him with hilarity, and then took his stand in the doorway.

The look of hunted terror in the man's face would have moved his bitterest foe to pity. He sat down helplessly on an empty packing-case which was lying where it had been flung, just outside the door, and looked at Nathan with haggard eyes. Nathan had ceased from his letter-writing and come to the doorway, because he did not care to be alone inside with Koos, after his last night's experience of being gripped. He stood in the doorway, whistling, and with his hands in his pockets. Then, after a pause—

"Well, Koos, old man, you look chippy to-day. What's up, eh?"

Koos stood up and again laid his hand on Nathan's shoulder. Nathan, however, had been prepared for this, so he slipped like an eel from under the huge hand that threatened to crush him, darted away to a distance of a few yards, and then wheeled round facing Koos, who was limping heavily after him with murder in his eye. He determined to risk something. He had planned out moves for the game he had to play. Here, in the full light of day and within sight of the whole of Namies, was the place to begin the struggle.

"Look here, Koos Bester," he said in a low tone, "if you think you are going to paw me about as you would a blasted Bushman, you are very much mistaken. Understand me now, once and for all—if ever you lay that leg-o'-mutton hand of yours on me again, I'll—I'll—Well, I won't say exactly what I'll do, but you can just look out for yourself—mind that."

Koos at once collapsed into abjectness. Nathan pursued his advantage—

"One would think it was *I* that had booted a blooming nigger to death. Where do you think you'd be if I were to split, eh?"

Here he attempted a somewhat conventional representation of the legal tragedy which follows the donning of the black cap by a certain high judicial functionary. In it his tongue, the whites of his eyes, his left hand, and the butt of his ear played conspicuous parts. Koos gasped and murmured unintelligibly. Nathan resumed—

"Now, look here, I'm not going to split—this is, if you are a good boy and do as you're told, and keep your paws to yourself. See?" Koos made a dismal attempt to smile, as though he regarded this as a pleasantry. He was now completely cowed, and would have set his neck under the foot of the man before him had he been told to do so.

He came close up to Nathan, cleared his throat, and whispered hoarsely—

"What did he tell your brother?"

"That's just what I don't know. My brother and I have had a blooming diplomatic difference; don't speak, you know. He actually appears to think that I've had a hand in this business;—as if your feet were not big enough to do your own kicking."

Koos gave a gasp of relief. His mind had become almost unnaturally alert under the strain upon it. If Max thought as Nathan said, it was clear that he knew nothing definite.

The unhappy man became conscious of the fact that he had not eaten since early on the previous day. A sudden hunger seized him; he felt like a wolf. He begged of Nathan to give him food. Nathan led the way into the shop, and there produced a loaf of bread, and some bultong which he took out of a sack under the counter. Koos seized greedily upon the food and ate with avidity. Nathan watched him narrowly. When he had finished eating Koos arose and left the shop. Max had just previously come in, so Nathan went out after Koos. He still felt a stiffness in his shoulder from the effects of last night's gripping. He shrugged it purposely until he felt a severe twinge. The pain was like salt for the feast of his revenge against the strong man who had hurt and insulted him.

"Well, old man, had a good feed?"

"Yes, I ate well."

"Yes, you seemed to enjoy your grub. I say, Koos, I've been thinking things over a bit, and I find I'll want a few more of those cattle of yours. What do you say to my taking another fifty head?"

Koos looked up. His alert senses had detected something unusual in the tone of Nathan's voice. Nathan had distinctly said that he did not require any more cattle.

"I'm thinking of taking another trip to Cape Town, and I thought you might just drive another lot down as far as Clanwilliam for me. What do you say?"

"Yes, you can have the cattle, but I cannot leave home just now; you will have to take them over at my camp."

"Well, old man—to oblige a friend, you know. I think you will be able, at all events, to send them on for me, eh?"

Nathan looked at Koos with such an amount of sinister meaning that the miserable Boer was filled with a vague sense of fresh dismay. Nathan continued—

"Look here, old man, I'll tell you what we'll do: we'll just drive down to your place to-morrow—across the dunes, you know—then we'll pick out the cattle and arrange about how you will send them down."

"But how can we cross the dunes? Your mules will never pull the cart through?"

"Quite right, old man; and that's why you are to drive me down in your own trap. You told me that you crossed the dunes as you came up, so you might as well go back the same way. See?"

"But how are you to get back here if you do not take your own cart?"

Nathan dug Koos playfully in the ribs, and then linked his skinny arm with the Boer's large limb.

"Well, how stupid of me not to have thought of that. Let's see—how can I get back, eh? Oh, I've just thought of a splendid plan: you'll drive me back too."

Koos gave a sidelong glance of such bitter hatred at the stunted figure at his side that, had Nathan seen it, he surely would have recognised the danger of the course he was pursuing. But Nathan supposed that the giant was quite cowed, that this Samson was completely shorn of his locks. In his preoccupation he forgot about the Pillars of Gaza.

His thoughts were far away. He was evolving complicated schemes, planning vast undertakings, which he meant to effect by means of this rough instrument, whose strength might be guided by his puny hand. He had reasoned it out—his theory as to the proper management of this tamed monster, and had come to the conclusion that curb, whip, and spur should be used upon him unsparingly, until he was thoroughly broken to harness.

Koos did not speak for a while. Then he said in a strained voice—

"If I take my horses again through the dunes this weather, they will be quite knocked up. You had better bring your own trap and mules, and we will go round the other way."

Nathan stood still, and his companion faced him. Then he repeated the pantomime in which his tongue, the whites of his eyes, and the butt of his ear were so suggestively in evidence. The face of Koos turned to the colour of ashes, and he trembled as though he had a fit of ague. Nathan again dug him playfully in the ribs.

"It's all right, old man, you need not get yourself into a state. I'm fond of you, Koos; I really am—in fact I wouldn't hurt you for the world. Besides, I'm very fond of your wife. Ain't she a pretty woman, eh? I say, Koos, did you ever see a man hanged?"

The Boer shook like an aspen through every fibre of his immense frame. His breath came in husky gasps.

"It's all right, old man," continued Nathan, "it's only my fun. We'll start to-morrow morning before it gets too hot, eh? Your horses will do it right enough. If the weather is very hot I'll get you to drive me back the other way. I'm not going to ask you to take me to Clanwilliam this time. I'm always willing to oblige a friend—ain't I, now?"

Just as night was falling Oom Schulpad went for a walk to the other side of the group of kopjes. It was dark when he returned, carrying a large armful of candle-bushes, which he had collected during the day and hidden in a safe place. He took these—not to the scherm belonging to the camp at which he was a guest, but to the deserted scherm formerly occupied by Gert Gemsbok. The scattered bushes of the scherm fence he rearranged, not against the wind but on the side facing the shop. He piled the candle-bushes upon the cold hearth and then stole quietly away.

Later, when the lights began to go out in the camps, he stepped quietly out of the mat-house, in which he was in the habit of sleeping, with his fiddle under his arm, and went softly up the hillside. When he reached the deserted scherm he laid himself down behind the rearranged fence, lit his pipe, and waited.

Koos Bester had no supper. After he had parted from Nathan he went and sat upon a rock a short distance from where his cart was standing. His horses were hobbled close by on the side of the kopje. He wanted their companionship during the interminable hours of the coming darkness.

His terrors of the supernatural had, for the moment, burnt themselves out. It was the sense of being subject to the ruthless bondage of Nathan which, just now, maddened him. He did not expect to sleep, but he thought he might be able to rest, wrapped in the regal quiet of the night.

When all was still, when the very last glimmer of light had disappeared from the camps, Koos arose and returned to his cart. He wrapped himself in his blanket and lay down between the wheels. His brain seemed to become a little cooler; the dulness of utter fatigue benumbed his faculties and mitigated his tribulation. He felt the gracious touch of the wing of Sleep across his eyelids. Surely God was taking pity on him—

A strange flicker of light rose and fell. What could it possibly mean? It came from the hillside above the shop. He must get up and see what it meant. Horror! a bright blaze was rising and falling in the scherm of the man he had slain. Yet, he tried to reason to himself, what nonsense to think that there was anything ghostly about the circumstance. No doubt some wandering—

His hair stood upon end and he shrieked aloud. From the scherm arose the notes of the air he knew so well. Struck from the strings, the pizzicato tones of the deadly tune seemed to run through his body until every nerve vibrated with the hateful sound. He rushed across the intervening space and beat with his fists against the iron door of Nathan's bedroom, until the whole building thundered.

Nathan sprang out of bed in deadly fear.

"Who is that, and what is the matter?" he called.

"Open, quick! It is I, Koos. Open, open!"

Nathan drew back the bolt and Koos sprang into the room, panting.

"I have seen his ghost—it is there in the scherm."

"Rot, Koos. Go to bed."

"It is there; go and see for yourself."

Nathan had no fear whatever of the supernatural. He slipped on a pair of shoes and came outside, followed by the trembling Boer. All was in darkness; not the faintest glimmer of light could be seen in the neighbourhood of the scherm, not a sound broke the stillness of the night.

"Why, you must have the 'rats,' Koos. Go to bed."

Koos begged humbly to be allowed to lie down on the floor in Nathan's room until morning. Nathan grumbled a bit, but at last consented to grant his request.

Chapter Thirteen.

"Whoso Diggeth a Pit..."

Next morning, just as day was breaking, Nathan and Koos Bester took their departure from Namies. Koos had not slept at all during the previous night. His face looked pinched and haggard, his hands trembled so that he was hardly capable of buckling the straps of the harness.

The morning was as pellucid as a dew-drop and the dunes looked preternaturally clear and distinct, the hollows being filled with amber-tinted shadow. The track lay like a narrow, coiling ribbon over the waste of plumy grass. The weird form of Bantom Berg arose gradually before the travellers like a warning finger, indicating the vast death-trap of which it is the centre, when, as the sun appeared above the horizon, its shafts smote suddenly as though a furnace-door had been suddenly opened. A short, hushing breath, as it were a gasp of apprehension of the fiery terrors of the day, seemed to pass westward over the Desert.

They reached a place called "Inkruip," and here it was decided to outspan and rest the team. The name is a literal translation into Dutch of a word in the Bushman tongue which means "creep in." A small stone kopje stands here, and in its side is a narrow passage through which an ordinary-sized man may just manage to force himself. A small chamber is then reached, and from this another passage leads. Into this one can only pass upon hands and knees. It rapidly gets narrower, and at length dips suddenly at an angle of about forty-five degrees for some ten feet. At the bottom is a little hollow, in which is always to be found a few pannikinfuls of beautifully clear, fresh water, which is icy cold. It takes, however, two people to obtain water at Inkruip, for the man who descends the sloping shaft cannot get out again unless he is assisted by some one who pulls him back by means of a reim tied round his feet.

The rocks on the western side of the little kopje still afforded a slight protection from the blazing sunlight. The two men crept close against a low, perpendicular ledge of rock, over which the rays of the terrible sun were slowly encroaching. The sand was so hot that the horses were unable to stand still, so they moved uneasily about in the vain hope of easing their scorching feet.

"My, but ain't it just sultry!" said Nathan. He had managed to squeeze his small body into a wedge of shade too small to accommodate the bulk of the Boer, who was largely exposed to the sun-glare.

Koos murmured an unintelligible reply. Nathan, in spite of the heat, felt in good form; he was determined to converse.

"My, but ain't it funny that a big, strong chap like you should have to do just as I tell you, eh?"

Nathan could not see his companion's face, so he went on garrulously—

"I'll tell you what I mean to do; I'm just going to have a jolly rest down at your camp for two or three days. You can go down to Gamoep and collect the stock; I'll stay behind and cheer up the missus, eh?"

Koos bit his lip till the blood came. His face, still averted from Nathan, turned almost purple; the veins of his temples appeared as though they would burst. Nathan went on—"You must excuse me, old man; I'm not a married man myself, and, what's more, I don't know that I ever will be, but I've often thought that a married man should keep no secrets from his wife. Don't you agree with me, eh?" Koos still maintained silence. "Well, silence gives consent, as the copybooks say, so I suppose you agree with me. That being so, and without for a moment wishing to say anything that might lead your thoughts back in an unpleasant direction—and I'm sure you'll see that it's only out of friendship that I ask it—which is: Did you tell your wife about that little spree the other day?"

"No," replied Koos hoarsely.

"Well, I think you've made a mistake in not doing so, and you must let me persuade you to tell your wife all about it as soon as we get to your camp. If you like you may put off telling her until the morning, but you'd better get it over, as the man said when he jumped on the back of the alligator."

"Why should I tell my wife?"

"Several reasons. One is that if she were to hear about the thing from any one else she would think you didn't trust her, don't you know. Another is that I have reason to suspect your wife doesn't like me quite as well as I like her, and I want her to know what a friend I've been to you all through this business. See?"

In the brain of Koos something seemed to snap. The tension at once ceased, and he breathed freely. Strange lights flickered before his eyes, and his ears were filled with extraordinary sounds. He seemed to live through hours of rather pleasant delirium in the course of a few seconds. The voice of Nathan recalled him to a sense of his surroundings. Then the lights and sounds were suddenly swept away, and the idea which had been born in the turmoil stood forth adult in terrible and ravishing nakedness. His thirsty soul drank deep at the cup of an awful hope, and the dunes seemed to blossom into a red-hot, infernal garden.

"Look here, old chap," continued the Jew, plucking at his companion's sleeve to emphasise what he said. "No nonsense, mind; you've got to tell your wife all about it. See?"

"I'll tell her."

"Yes; and tell her, too, that she's got to make me jolly comfortable while you're away; and, in fact, to do every blessed thing I tell her. See?"

"Yes; I'll tell her all that."

"Now that's the way I like to hear you talk—nice and friendly, you know. I can see we're going to be good friends right enough. I'll not be hard on you, Koos; and if you do all I want you to, we'll both be quite happy. See?"

Koos replied in an even, cheerful voice that he would do all he possibly could to meet Nathan's wishes in everything. Nathan said—quite voluntarily—that if the weather continued hot he would not insist on being driven back through the dunes; he would submit to the inconvenience of a two-days' journey round by Puffadder instead. Koos expressed himself as being appropriately grateful for this evidence of consideration.

Cordiality being thus restored, the two chatted in the friendliest manner. In fact one would have thought that the mutually satisfactory relations of a week previously had never been interrupted.

When the time came to make another start, Nathan asked Koos to excuse him from getting up and helping to inspan, so Koos went around the kopje to where the cart stood and laid out the harness ready to be placed upon the horses.

Koos carried back to the cart from the kopje the little keg of water which had been placed in the shade. No one ever dreams of entering Bushmanland without at least one of such kegs. He had taken some pains to persuade Nathan against drinking more than a mere sip. Nathan, being accustomed to travelling in the Desert, knew that this was good advice, however hard to follow; that one should never touch water if one can avoid it whilst exposed to the rays of a hot sun. Nathan was extremely proud of the self-command which he evinced in following the advice, for he was very thirsty indeed and would have given a lot for a deep drink of something cool.

But Koos did a very curious thing after he had laid the harness out; he scraped a hole in the red-hot sand with his foot, and into this he poured every drop of the contents of the little keg. He need not have taken the trouble to scrape the hole, for the thirsty sand drank up the water as quickly as if it had been poured into space over the edge of the car of a balloon. However, there is nothing like being systematic when one has important work in hand. He stowed away the empty keg under the seat of the cart, and then went to fetch the horses.

These poor animals were standing, only a few hundred yards away, perched like so many goats upon a low ledge of light-coloured stone. This was more bearable to their feet than the red, scorching sand. The docile, well-trained brutes stood still until Koos went up and caught them. He laughed so heartily that the tears streamed down his cheeks, and he was hardly able to untie the hobble-knots from the forelegs of the youngest horse, which, being given to roaming, it was always necessary to secure. He led the horses back to the cart, and in a few minutes they stood in the traces uneasily shifting their feet from time to time, and looking round impatiently for the signal to start. Koos called to Nathan, who came forward and took his place, with many groanings, upon the hard, unprotected seat of the vehicle.

A start was made. Nathan seemed to fry in the heat. There was no longer a track, for whenever the wind blew the ever-shifting sand would have obliterated the trail of an army in an hour. Koos, however, knew every turn and changing fold in the limbs of the dune-monster, and took advantage of each depression, enabling him to force through one after another of the interminable series of tentacle-like ridges at its most vulnerable point.

The heat was indescribable. The horses broke into a lather of sweat at every ascent. This at once dried into adhesive flakes of white paste whenever the course led downhill. Nathan suffered increasing agonies from thirst, but he still listened to the persuasions of his companion against drinking whilst in the hot sunlight, and thus relaxing his pores until every drop of moisture drained out of his body. He accordingly, with increased admiration for his own powers of endurance, determined to hold out to the last extremity. From his manner it might have been supposed that this exercise of obvious discretion for his own advantage was really a something which Koos ought to have been extremely grateful for.

Twenty torrid miles of the dune-ground had to be travelled; on a day such as this, better fifty in the open Desert. After they had covered about eight miles, Nathan found his thirst absolutely intolerable, so he made Koos stop the cart and get the keg out from under the seat.

"Allemagtig!" exclaimed Koos, "the keg is empty!"

"Empty!" shrieked Nathan in agony. "Then I'll die of thirst. Look here, you damned murdering hound; I'll make you swing for this."

Koos replied to the effect that he was very sorry; he supposed the cork must have sprung out from the jolting. Nathan's moods alternated between the whimperingly pathetic and the impotently furious; his words, between blasphemous revilings and minor-keyed entreaties. Koos did his best to comfort him, promising water within two hours at the most.

The course now led up a deep and narrow passage between two branches which were rooted in the main dune almost at the same point, and which ran parallel for several miles. One of these had to be crossed close to its point of origin at a spot where it curved slightly, and where the winds had blown a shallow gap. This locality was like the innermost circle of hell. As the horses bravely struggled up to the gap through the scorching sand, into which they sank above their fetlocks, Koos leaped out of the cart so as to ease the strain, and asked Nathan to do the same. Nathan, however, plaintively declined, saying that he could not walk ten yards in the sand.

They reached the top of the ascent, and Koos stopped the horses for the purpose of giving them a blow. Then he climbed into the cart and took his seat beside his suffering companion. After they had rested for a couple of minutes, Nathan said, in tones of husky despair—

"Go on, Koos, for God's sake! I'm dying of thirst!"

Koos gathered the reins up preparatory to making a start. Then he asked Nathan to stand up for a moment so that he might adjust the seat. Nathan, groaning, leant forward and crouched with his hands on the splash-board. Koos seized him between his huge hands, lifted him high with a wrench, and flung him down the side of the dune.

The reins he had gripped between his knees, the whip stood ready at his hand. In a moment the team, refreshed by the short pause, were dragging the cart down the side of the dune at a floundering gallop.

After going for about two hundred yards Koos hauled the horses back almost upon their haunches, and the cart suddenly stopped. He looked round; Nathan was stumbling slowly down the sandy slope, falling every few yards. Koos allowed him to come to within about fifty yards of the cart, and then he urged the horses into a walk. Nathan made a desperate effort and broke into a staggering run, which somewhat decreased the distance. Koos then whipped the horses into a trot, and he heard behind him a hoarse and stifled cry as of a wild beast in agony. After a few minutes he again pulled the team into a walk and looked back. A motionless figure lay huddled with its face upon the sand.

Koos uttered a wild laugh, frightful to hear, and urged the horses forward at a mad gallop.

Chapter Fourteen.

The Nachtmaal, and After.

A few days after the departure of Nathan and Koos Bester the great annual event, the visit of the pastor of the Dutch Reformed Church to Namies, took place.

The Reverend Nicholas Joubert, who resided at Garies, two hundred miles as the crow flies, across the Desert, made a tour through Bushmanland every autumn. He travelled in his own comfortably appointed spring-wagon, teams of horses for which were provided by the more well-to-do among the Trek-Boers, as relays along a prescribed course.

The Trek-Boers congregated at the different water-places to meet the pastor. Services would be held, catechisings instituted, confirmations, marriages, and christenings solemnised.

Namies, if the summer rains happen to have been copious, is the great assembling-place for the Trek-Boers of Northern Bushmanland; in fact, several dozen camps may be seen grouped around the kopjes on these occasions, and the pastor has known what it is to preach there to several hundred souls.

There is little that is distinctive about these meetings. Enthusiasm is not an element in them, for the Boer, and more especially the Trek-Boer, takes his religion, like everything else, quietly and without passion or excitement. The sermons are mainly theological, the prayers are extremely long, the Old Testament is more in evidence than the New, the singing of the psalms and hymns is nasal, and extremely trying to any one with a musical ear.

This species of religious gathering is known as the "Nachtmaal," which is the Dutch equivalent for the Lord's Supper. In the more civilised districts the Boers gather from far and near around the different church-buildings four times annually. In Bushmanland, however, no church-buildings exist, so the pastor gathers his wandering sheep together once in every year, usually in autumn, but of course the time must be determined by the rains. They are thus kept in touch with the formal observances of their professed religion.

It is a strange and motley gathering which one sees under the awning of "buck-sails," as the canvas overalls of the wagons are called, stretched over poles. Probably the assemblage contains a larger proportion of unattractive female countenances than one would find in any other collection of Caucasians. Here and there, however, one may notice a strangely beautiful face shining like a fresh lily between withered cabbages. Among the faces of the men one notices many diverse types. Some show a rugged nobility that would ensure their owners a fair livelihood in any city where art is followed. The most salient characteristic of both men and women is the listlessness of attitude as well as of expression.

All were wondering at Nathan's absence; for obvious reasons he always made a point of being present at the Nachtmaal. This is the great time for squaring off accounts, for bartering piles of hides, jackal-skins, and karosses, the latter made by the deft fingers of the Boer women from the skins of the fat-tailed sheep, as well as from those of wild animals. Nathan had left no instructions; he had even taken the keys of the little iron safe in which the promissory notes, "good-fors," and acknowledgments of debt which the Boers had signed from time to time to cover their accounts, were kept. Such transactions involved a ruinous rate of interest for the accommodation granted, and were generally made payable at Nachtmaal-time. Max knew that Nathan had an unusually large number of these on hand. On several grounds Nathan's absence was absolutely unaccountable.

As the Trek-Boers assembled from far and near Max had a busy time of it. It seemed to be a *sine qua non* among the Boers that each individual should have at least one new article noticeable in his or her attire at the Nachtmaal. It was customary for Max to nail down the flap of the counter at Nachtmaal-time, so as to prevent the women, many of whom are incorrigible pilferers, from crowding round beneath the shelves and "snapping up unconsidered trifles."

Sunday passed with its almost interminable services, and on Monday Maria and Petronella were united in marriage to their respective swains. The weddings were only two among some dozen or so. These were, however, the most notable—one would hardly use the term "fashionable."

The brides were attired in white muslin frocks and pale green sashes. A single wreath of orange-blossoms was divided between them. The bridegrooms levied contributions on several friends for the black broadcloth attire in which they were wed. Black broadcloth, largely irrespective of fit, represents the Boer ideal of the perfection of male garb.

In the evening something remotely approaching a jollification was held at the Hattingh camp. Next to Old Schalk's wagon stood another, which had been borrowed for the occasion, and between the tent-frames of these vehicles some of the buck-sails, which had formed the roof of the extemporised church of the previous day, were stretched. In the space thus covered in the company sat whilst innumerable cups of coffee were handed round. Mynheer, the minister, came and remained for about half an hour. After he had taken his departure for his wagon, which was outspanned on the other side of the kopjes, Oom Schulpad produced his violin and struck up a lively polka.

Dancing was, of course, out of the question under the awning on account of the sand. In the large mat-house and in the tent, however, the floors had been hardened by use. The contents of these edifices were soon removed and piled outside, and a few couples forthwith began dancing. Each respective bride and bridegroom danced exclusively one with the other, and the couples who stood up at first remained, as a rule, partners for the whole evening.

At the conclusion of each dance the couples in possession of the limited spaces came outside and seated themselves under the awning, thus making room for another relay. The only lights came from a few dip candles, and the dust kicked up from loose floors hung about in thick clouds. Dancing was carried on in a silent, business-like manner, each lady holding her partner with interlocked fingers behind his neck, whilst he passed his arms around her substantial body just below the armpits, and clasped his hands behind her back.

Susannah refused to dance; she and Max sat together just outside the awning, listening to the music. Oom Schulpad sat playing between the mat-house and the tent, so that the polkas could be heard equally well in both.

Old Schalk sat in his chair under the awning and talked oracularly to an attentive circle. His wife, fatigued from the exertions of the day, had collapsed on a stool in the scherm, from which she continually dispensed coffee, with the assistance of the Hottentot maids.

"I wonder where Koos Bester is," said Oom Dantje van Rooyen; "I never knew him miss a Nachtmaal before."

"I passed his camp on Thursday," said a Boer from the eastward, "and his wife told me that he was lying sick in the mat-house."

"Did she say what was the matter with him?" asked Old Schalk.

"Yes; she said it was pains in his head, and that he could not sleep and would not eat or speak. Did you hear that he killed two of his horses when going through the dunes after he left here? They died just after he reached home."

"No, I didn't hear that. Was Nathan at the camp?"

"No, I heard nothing of Nathan."

"That is strange; he and Koos left here last Friday week."

"How can that be, then? My son Diedrik met Koos driving home from the dunes on Friday evening, and he was alone."

Old Schalk smoked in silence for a few moments; then he called to Max, who came in immediately.

"Max, have you heard when Nathan is coming back?"

"No, Oom, I have heard nothing of him since he left here with Koos Bester."

"That was on Friday week, eh?"

"Ja, Oom."

Old Schalk smoked for a long time in silence; Max rejoined Susannah outside. One by one the male guests arose from their seats and left the awning. Outside they collected in two or three groups and conversed in whispers. Diederik, the young Boer who had been referred to in the conversation with Oom Dantje van Rooyen, was called from the mat-house, where he was dancing.

Diederik repeated his story. He had, undoubtedly, seen Koos Bester driving alone from the direction of the dunes on the evening of the day upon which Koos and Nathan left Namies. Although not spoken of, it was well known that Koos Bester had killed Gert Gemsbok, and every one had noticed the strangeness of Koos' manner ever since.

A shadow of apprehension seemed to have fallen on the company. Men glanced up in silence and read in each other's eyes their own ominous thoughts. Max noticed the change which had come over the others, and inquired as to the reason. Old Schalk sent again for him, and quietly told him the facts as they stood, and left him to draw his own deductions.

At midnight the newly married couples were escorted to their respective wagons, which were standing within a short distance of each other, by a party of young men and maidens. After some uncouth romping and unrefined jokes the escort returned to the Hattingh camp. Contrary to usage the party broke up at once, the different families returning to their respective camps, silent, or whispering to each other the forebodings which they felt.

Afterwards a few of the Boers met as a sort of informal council to discuss the situation and decide as to what was best to be done under the circumstances. The meeting took place at the Hattingh camp, and Max was present. It was settled that a party of six men should start at once for Inkruip. After resting there until daylight they would take on the spoor of the cart through the dunes. The dune route being the shortest cut to Koos Bester's camp, there was no necessity for sending a party round by the road.

Of course the most urgently necessary thing to do was to interrogate Koos himself. The wind had not blown with any degree of violence since the date of the departure of the missing man, so there would be no difficulty in finding and following the spoor.

During the discussion several very suspicious circumstances came to light. These were all more or less trifles, but, under the circumstances, they became significant. One had noticed Koos walking by himself, muttering, and with hands convulsively clenched. Another had seen him look at Nathan with a terrible expression. Then the killing of the horses. It was well known that Nathan had been in Koos' company when Gert Gemsbok had been killed. Over and over again the young man who had passed Koos on his way from the dunes was interrogated and cross-examined, but his story could not be shaken. Every one felt satisfied that a tragedy had taken place, and was eager to clear up the mystery.

Within an hour the party, under the leadership of Oom Dantje van Rooyen—who rode the identical horse that was supposed to have killed Gert Gemsbok—had started. Inkruip was reached shortly before dawn. Here a halt was made. The most slender man was made to go down the inclined shaft for the purpose of filling the water-bottles. At the first glimmer of dawn the saddles were again placed upon the horses.

The spoor of the cart lay as clearly defined as if it had only been made on the previous day. It is a peculiarity of the Desert sand that if the wind has not happened to blow hard it retains a spoor distinctly for weeks, or even months.

Shortly after starting it was found that the ordinary course through the dunes had been departed from; the spoor trended away to the left, towards Bantom Berg, and led through a tract which, according to the patriarch of the party, had never been crossed by a vehicle before.

"Allemachtig!" said Oom Dantje, as he ploughed through sand which nearly reached his horse's knees, "no wonder he killed two of his team!"

More and more the spoor trended towards Bantom Berg. The day was cool, a light breeze blowing from the south, so neither men nor horses were much distressed. Suddenly the spoor curved towards a gap in the right-hand dune. In climbing to this the men, with one accord, dismounted from their horses. When they reached the middle of the gap they stood still to recover breath.

"Look there," said Oom Dantje, pointing to a couple of jackals slinking off into a small patch of scrub about two hundred yards ahead.

"Yes, and there are the ears of another sticking out over that tuft," said one of the men.

They moved slowly on. As they did so they saw several more jackals. These trotted or slunk away to right and left. Oom Dantje reined in his horse and raised his hand as a sign to the others to pause. Then he pointed to what appeared to be fragments of torn clothing scattered about on the sand at each side of the track. They rode a little nearer, but again paused—with one accord this time, for under the surrounding bushes, whither they had been dragged by the jackals, they saw the scattered bones of a human body.

There was no doubt as to the identity of the remains. The different articles of clothing were well known as having belonged to Nathan. Every fragment was carefully gathered up and placed in a sack which one of the men had been using as a saddlecloth. A pocket-book containing papers, a bunch of keys and a silver watch, were also found. These were carefully placed in a saddle-bag.

The gruesome bundle was tied across the saddle upon one of the horses, and the cavalcade started back for Namies, the men dismounting by turns to give a lift to the man who had lent his horse for the purpose of carrying the remains. It was nearly midnight when they reached Namies.

Old Schalk at once woke to sense of his duty as Assistant Field Cornet. Within half an hour a mounted messenger was on his way to the Special Magistrate with a quaintly scrawled report of the case.

Max was sent for. He stood over the sack which contained the mortal remains of his brother with a very white, scared face. He was filled with horror, but felt no grief. The dead man had earned his brother's hatred and contempt. Max did not pretend for a moment that he felt any sorrow. He could not but feel that the fate which had befallen one whom he instinctively knew was responsible to a great extent for a foul murder committed on an innocent fellow-creature was largely deserved.

Within a quarter of an hour almost every inhabitant of Namies was at the Hattingh camp. Old Schalk sat on his chair and propounded oracularly his views upon the occurrence to all and sundry. A fire was lit—kettles, pannikins, and other requisites were fetched from the surrounding camps, and a sort of coffee-parliament held session until long after sunrise.

The sack containing the horror had not been opened, pending the arrival of the Special Magistrate; it was hung in the fork of a high koekerboom about fifty yards away. Towards this tree which bore such terrible fruit furtive and frightened glances were shot from time to time. The children, who had crept out and joined the elders, cowered in terror against the latter's legs whilst the darkness lasted. After daylight had come, curiosity got the better of fright, and they crept out and took up positions in small groups around the koekerboom, but at a respectful distance. For hours they silently gazed, wide-eyed and fascinated, at the Thing which hung in its fork, lifted thereto by its own act when a sentient being, even as Haman of old was hung upon the high gallows which he had prepared for Mordecai.

Chapter Fifteen.

"Whoso Breaketh a Fence..."

The night had just fallen when Koos Bester arrived at his camp after leaving Nathan, his persecutor, to his dreadful fate in the burning dunes. Koos arrived in the wildest state of excitement and the highest of spirits. His team was in a miserable condition; the poor horses just staggered away for a few yards when outspanned and then sank exhausted on the ground. The Hottentot servants attempted to make them get up and walk slowly about so as to cool gradually before drinking. With some difficulty the leaders were got upon their legs. The wheelers, however, could not be induced by either blows or persuasion to arise; about an hour afterwards it was found that they were dead.

Mrs Bester was very uneasy; she felt that something was wrong. Koos drank quantities of water but could not be induced to eat. After a while he flung himself upon the bed and fell at once into a deep sleep which lasted until noon of the following day. Then he became violently ill. At his wife's earnest solicitation he had eaten a little food upon awakening, but this he was unable to keep upon his stomach. Then he lay on the bed for a couple of days, during which he hardly spoke.

All the other Boers had trekked away to the Nachtmaal at Namies, so, with the exception of her old and feeble father and the Hottentot servants, Mrs Bester had no one to turn to for assistance or advice.

One night Koos began muttering to himself; from this time he seemed to be quite bereft of his understanding. He sometimes ate food that was placed before him with avidity. Six days and nights passed in this manner. He appeared to suffer acute pain in his head and to be continually thirsty. At length he again slept deeply. Mrs Bester had taken the children out of the mat-house and was staying with them in the wagon for the purpose of keeping them quiet. In the middle of the night she stole quietly out and went on tiptoe to the mat-house door. She listened carefully, but there was no sound of breathing. Then she softly struck a match and looked in under the door-flap. The bed was empty. She called up the servants and a search was made, but no trace of her husband could be found.

Koos Bester awoke just before midnight and sat up in bed. He could not remember where he was or what had happened. He got up and groped about; then he realised that he was at home, in his own mat-house. Then the past came back to him, bit by bit, and the wretched man realised that he had stained his soul with a double murder. He would be hanged, that was now certain; he would give himself up and get the thing over as soon as possible. To get it over quickly was all he was very anxious about.

But where were his wife and children? Some faint flickering memories of what had occurred during his delirium came back to him, and he arrived at a true inference regarding their absence. He was glad. It was terrible to be alone, but the dread of meeting his wife and telling her—as he felt he inevitably must when next he saw her—of what he had done, kept him from calling her. He felt quite sure that she and the children were in the wagon, close at hand.

The darkness was full of terrible and menacing shapes; huddled figures crouched all over the floor. The far, faint yowl of a jackal sounded from the direction of the dunes; it reminded him of Nathan's hoarse, despairing scream when he realised that he was abandoned to die of thirst. The mat-house, with its population of mysterious shadows and huddled shapes, became intolerable. Better the sense of freedom outside under the accusing stars, where a man can get away from the thing that seems to crawl to his feet as though to clasp his knees. He lifted the door-flap and stepped out into the night.

The Hottentot servants had inhabited a scherm about fifty yards to the rear of the camp. Hottentots often sit up more than half the night, chatting, laughing, and dancing. Mrs Bester, for the sake of keeping the neighbourhood quiet, had told the servants to move their scherm farther away. They had, accordingly, taken their belongings to the other side of a little knoll about two hundred yards away, on the right-hand side of the camp. Here they might hold their nocturnal jollifications to their hearts' content without disturbing anybody or anything except the meerkats in the adjacent burrows.

A wandering stranger from Great Namaqualand had arrived during the course of the evening. This man had a ramkee upon which he performed with skill. A few months previously he had visited Namies, and had one night listened to Gert Gemsbok playing his favourite tune. Being struck with admiration of the melody, he had picked it up. He was now popularising it among the dwellers of the Desert, for he played it at every scherm he visited.

Coffee had been made of burnt rye, a sheep had died on the previous day; thus the scherm contained the materials for a feast. The company had been dancing to a series of inspiriting reels, but were now resting a space from their laborious leapings and gruntings. The stranger was playing Gert Gemsbok's tune as an interlude to the reels. A bright fire of candle-bushes was burning. All but the ramkee player were lying down resting behind the scherm fence.

When Koos Bester stepped out of the mat-house he at once experienced a sense of relief. His head was bare and the cool breeze which wandered over the Desert refreshed his brain. The stars could, he found, pity as well as accuse; the night seemed to take compassion on his misery. He looked round to the back of the camp in the direction of where the scherm of the servants had been, and was relieved to see no light. He wanted to be free—even of the suggestion of the presence of another human being—until he had rearranged his distorted faculties. The sandy road led past the camp; he turned to the right and paced slowly along it, with bent head.

He stopped short, for a sound of horribly familiar music reached his ear; then he started and gasped, for the glow of a fire smote his eyes, coming from behind the little knoll. Being to windward of the knoll, he could not exactly distinguish what tune was being played. He knew that the instrument was a ramkee—that, in itself, was sufficiently horrible. A cold hand seemed to steal into his breast and gradually close upon his stricken heart. He stood rigidly still and tried to catch the tune exactly. He strained every nerve with this end, but the breeze freshened slightly, and only an indefinite tinkle reached him. In the midst of his reeling consciousness only one idea stood firm—he must go closer and determine who the player was and what the tune that was being played. He pressed his hands convulsively to his ears and stepped, crouching, towards the knoll.

He reached the knoll and cautiously raised his head till he was able to see over its top. The musician was sitting with his back towards the watcher, and just inside the scherm. Against the diffused glow of the embers—for the flame had died down—the outline of his head and shoulders stood clear and black. To the mind of Koos came the certain conviction that he was looking at the ghost of the man he had murdered. With a supreme effort of despairing will he tore his shielding hands away from his ears, and the unmistakable tones of the dead man's music crashed like thunder into his brain.

Then Koos Bester's madness returned upon him, and he fled away noiselessly across the Desert sands in the direction of the dunes.

It was long before he paused, for the fever in his brain prevented him from feeling fatigue. At length, as he was running over the roofs of a city of Desert mice, the ground gave way beneath his foot and he fell. The shock rendered him almost senseless. After a few minutes he sat up, pressed his hands to his temples, and began to grope in the haunted spaces of his darkened intellect for some clue to guide him.

He looked around. The dew-washed air of the Desert night was clear as crystal, the pulsing stars were domed over him sumptuously. He dug his hot hands into the cooling sand and lifted his faced to meet the soft, refreshing breeze.

The Hottentots at the scherm had evidently thrown another armful of candle-bush upon the embers, for a bright flame shot up and momentarily increased in volume. Koos gazed at it, fascinated. As the fire grew brighter he thought it was rushing toward him with terrific speed. The flames had been sent from hell to consume him quick. Like Abiram, God had doomed him for his crimes to go down alive into the pit. He sprang to his feet with a terrible cry, and again fled onwards in the direction of the dunes.

When he again paused he was wading in the heavy sand on the flank of the main dune. He had ascended slightly and thus could overlook a large area of the Desert. The cold breath which circles around the world as the precursor of the dawn was stealing over the plains. The rain had fallen recently upon this side of the Desert, and many of the Boers had sent their stock, in charge of herds, to graze on the track of the shower. The scantily clad Hottentots awoke to the chill, so they began to light fires. Here and there, at immense distances apart, he could see the sudden leapings of the flames from the easily kindled candle-bushes. To the demented brain of the fugitive it appeared as if the whole Desert were full of fiends seeking him with torches, far and near. Where the Milky Way dipped to the horizon the thronging stars seemed each a torch lit at the nether flame, and borne by a searching demon. In among the sinuous dunes he might escape. If he could but reach Inkruip he might creep down the water-shaft and hide. They would never think of looking for him there. In the icy water he might cool his scorched brain.

He stumbled on, crossing dune after dune and ploughing through the sand as with the strength of a giant. In one of the hollows he came to a clump of low bush. Into this he crept for hiding. He lay prone, completely covered, and looking out through a narrow opening. The morning star tipped the back of the dune he had last crossed and thrilled through the clear atmosphere with almost super-stellar brilliance. Koos took this for the torch of a tracking fiend, and again rushed forward with a scream of agonised dismay. His only possible refuge now was under the ground at Inkruip.

The sun arose and scorched his bare head. He was now almost unconscious; he simply pressed forward in obedience to a blind, animal instinct—a sort of momentum generated by the terror which had passed away with the darkness.

It was an awful day, not a breath of wind could be felt, but the sun smote down from a pitiless heaven in all the fulness of its torrid might. Koos pressed blindly up the side of a steep, high dune—his breath coming in husky, choking gasps. Then something seemed to explode in his head with the sound like that of a cannon, and he fell upon his face in the sand.

He had one blinding flash of consciousness, during the continuance of which he seemed again to live through all his lifetime and see anew everything he had ever seen. The minutest trifles of former experience became distinctly apparent, as the smallest details of a landscape show up when lightning flashes near and vividly on a dark night. Then came the darkness which men call death.

As soon as ever day broke the spoor of the missing man was found and followed. Mrs Bester, assisted by her old father, inspanned four horses in the cart and drove on behind the trackers. When she reached the dunes she found that the horses could take the cart no farther, so she outspanned the team and tied the legs of each animal together to prevent it from straying.

She sat through weary hours in the broiling heat. Early in the afternoon one of the Hottentots returned with word that her husband's dead body had been found. The horses were at once inspanned, and the cart taken by a roundabout course to the vicinity of where it was lying. It was late at night when she arrived at the camp, with the corpse of her husband tied, stiff and stark, on the seat beside her.

Next day two constables came with a warrant for Koos Bester's arrest, but he had gone before a higher tribunal than that of the Special Magistrate.

Chapter Sixteen.

A Conversion, a Wedding, and several other Things.

Max, being heir to his brother's estate, was now well off. Old Schalk, mindful of his account as standing in the books at the shop, felt obliged to be civil. Max was, and felt himself to be, master of the situation.

No longer the shy, diffident dreamer of a few months back, Max developed a keenness and aptitude for business which came as an unpleasant revelation to those who tried to get on his blind side. In fact Max had no blind side—he seemed to have eyes all round his head.

He soon satisfied himself of one thing, namely, that a business such as his, unless the legitimate gains were supplemented by the profits of the illicit trade in wild ostrich feathers, would not pay at Namies. Not seeing his way towards following Nathan's dangerous methods, he determined to wind up the business as it stood, and reopen in some spot in Southern Bushmanland were the farmers were in better circumstances, and where communication with more civilised parts was neither so difficult nor so uncertain. However, he kept these conclusions strictly to himself.

There was one drawer in the little iron safe of which Nathan had always kept the key. Upon opening this he found, to his astonishment, documents which showed that there was a balance to his credit in one of the Cape Town banks of over a thousand pounds, and that the stock, which was worth several hundreds more, was fully paid for. He was a rich man. The diamonds were worth a considerable amount—but these he would have to keep until he could go to Europe before he could realise them.

Amid the flux and reformation of his character his love for Susannah never changed. It was probably owing to this that he did not, under his recent experiences, lose all faith in human nature. He now felt that he was in such a position that he could marry whenever he wanted to. As a measure of policy he allowed, at this juncture, the Hattinghs to have a little more credit, and the quality of the coffee dispensed so lavishly by Mrs Hattingh from the scherm—to all comers—improved very much in consequence. He made up his mind that as soon as Susannah became his wife he would write off the whole of the Hattingh account as a bad debt, and afterwards take care that no further credit was given in that quarter.

"I will marry you as soon as ever you like," said Susannah to him one day; "but you must first become a Christian; then I know Uncle will not refuse."

Max had not the slightest objection to doing this. He had left his people when but a child, and had thus never acquired that pride of race which so distinguishes the average Jew, and which often causes him to cleave passionately to the observances of that religion which still keeps Israel a separate people, even after all faith in dogma may have perished.

Max had come in contact with no Jews except Nathan and others of his class. These had earned the young man's unmitigated contempt. As to Christianity—he looked upon its profession as a mere matter of convenience. The only Christians whom he knew were very sincere in their faith, and would have looked upon any one harbouring the slightest religious doubt as being worse than heathen Bushmen, yet their religion did not appear to have the slightest effect upon their conduct. The case of poor old Gert Gemsbok had set Max thinking deeply upon these matters, and the conclusions he arrived at were only negative ones.

The mind of Max, from utter want of culture, was probably not well fitted to deal with the higher problems. Had it been so he might easily have seen that the so-called Christians who inhabited Bushmanland were really far more like Jews than the worshippers in any modern synagogue on Saturday, for they looked upon themselves as the Almighty's chosen people, and felt that the heathen had been given to them as their inheritance, even as the

Hittites, the Hivites, and other unhappy tribes had been given for spoiling unto the followers of Moses. In this essential of all Christianity worth the name the love of one's kind, irrespective of colour or class, the Boer certainly fails. On the other hand, his attitude towards the inferior race is almost exactly that of the Old Testament Jew, with, however, one important reservation—he does not look upon it as a sacred duty to destroy them, nor does he do so unless he considers that they have provoked destruction by refusing to obey his behests.

Max possessed a useful native faculty for arranging evidence, digesting it, and deciding impartially thereon. He brought this faculty to bear upon the question of religion, with the result that he made up his mind that the two religions he had had some experience of were equally true and equally false. Certainly he had very little evidence, one way or another, to go upon. His surroundings, rather than he, were responsible for this. Probably, moreover, the religious sense was absent from his organisation. His natural impulses were good, he had no ideals or aspirations. He looked upon most of the people with whom he came in contact with a kind of mild contempt. He saw clearly in them weaknesses of which he himself was free. Thus, without being in any way conceited, he felt instinctively that he was superior to the generality of those he met.

Life with Susannah appeared good to him, and he would not let the faint and mainly instinctive scruples which he felt about professing a religion he did not believe in, stand in the way of the realisation of his happiness. So he borrowed a Catechism of the Dutch Reformed Church from Old Schalk and began to read up towards his conversion.

He found that without any further explanations he had come to be looked upon as Susannah's accepted lover. It was, of course, assumed that he was to be baptised and received as a Church member as soon as possible.

By collusion with Mrs Hattingh he managed so that some feminine habiliments of very superior quality, which came with his last consignment of goods from Cape Town, were purchased for Susannah. Her lover had, accordingly, the pleasure of at length seeing Susannah dressed in a manner which did something like justice to her beauty.

Max caused two commodious mat-houses to be put up at the back of the shop, on the site of poor old Gemsbok's scherm. These he furnished simply but comfortably.

In the course of a few months the Reverend Nicholas Joubert received a call at Garies from a young Jew, who stated that he had abjured the errors of Judaism and wished to embrace the Christian faith. Although his face seemed familiar, Mr Joubert did not at first recognise the convert. However, he eventually recalled—or said that he recalled—having seen him at Namies. As the convert stated that the services held by Mr Joubert were the only Christian ones he had ever been present at, the minister naturally enough attributed this remarkable conversion to the efficacy of his own personal ministrations, and was favourably disposed to the neophyte accordingly—especially as the latter answered all questions put to him most discreetly and knew his Catechism so well. No obstacles intervening, the preliminary steps towards Church membership were at once taken, and Max returned without delay to Namies.

He took back with him some books, with the contents of which he had to make himself familiar. Before leaving he made an arrangement of terms in which the minister, for a consideration, agreed to make his next visit to Bushmanland at a much earlier date than usual, and to solemnise a certain confirmation and a wedding—the confirmed party being the bridegroom—on the same day.

This programme was carried out. Max and Susannah were married. There were very few Boers in the vicinity of Namies just then, so the wedding was an extremely quiet affair. The short honeymoon was spent in Old Schalk's wagon (lent for the occasion) at Agenhuis, a water-place about forty miles away. In the midst of his raptures Max found time to effect a favourable deal in fat-tailed sheep, which were just then very much in demand by the travelling agents of the Cape Town butchers.

Very soon after his marriage Max began to make arrangements for winding up his business. He had heard of a spot on the southern margin of the Desert where rains fell with comparative regularity, and where a profitable trade might be done in salt from the neighbouring "pans." Here he determined to establish a business. Old Schalk did not like the idea of his leaving Namies, but Susannah raised no objection whatever to his doing so.

It is not many years since all this happened. To-day, at a certain place where there is a well which affords a copious supply of very pure water, in the northern part of the Calvinia Division, there stands a small but comfortable house built of red brick. Over the front door is a signboard bearing the legend: "Max Steinmetz, Allegemene Handelaar en Produkten Kooper." ("General Dealer and Produce Buyer.") Behind the counter you may see Max, and sometimes Susannah. Playing about outside, whenever the weather is cool enough, may be noticed several small, dark-eyed children of remarkable beauty. Max has changed in appearance more than Susannah. The sedentary life and close application to business has made his shoulders stoop somewhat and given deepening lines to his face. He is still handsome, but, somehow, one feels that Raphael would no longer have cared to paint his portrait.

Susannah is as pretty as ever, and has acquired a touch of refinement which was wanting before. On the other hand, her features have a suspicion of dawning sharpness which they lacked in the old days at Namies.

Max has prospered. The moral trade in salt gives smaller profits than did the immoral trade in wild ostrich feathers, but it is safe, and there is no heavy legal penalty hanging like a Damocles sword over the head of the trader. The business now supports a clerk—a young Englishman of good education but indifferent lungs, and who was ordered a karoo climate by the doctors.

It is the rule of the Steinmetz household that nothing but the English language shall be spoken—unless when there happen to be Dutch guests present. Susannah is thus rapidly acquiring a knowledge of her husband's mother-tongue. To this end Max encourages her to read English books, and he corrects, in private, the faults of her speech.

Max still has the diamonds in his safe. He means some day to take them to England. If, however, his business continues to prosper at the same rate as during the past few years, there is at least a chance of his not disposing of them. It may be—for Max has a sound instinctive knowledge of human nature—that he will have them cut and made into a necklace, and that he may attempt to bribe Susannah with this to reconsider her decision never to leave her beloved Bushmanland. Max knows that Susannah has an extremely pretty neck; what is more, she knows it too—moreover, he knows that she knows it.

If Susannah's command of the English language improves, it is quite possible that the effect of the necklet may be all that Max desires.

Bultong.—Dried meat.

Cartel.—A framework of wood, filled in with laced thongs. It is usually slung in the tent of a wagon, but is occasionally fixed upon forked sticks driven into the ground, and used as a bedstead.

Kaross.—A rug made of brayed skins.

Kloof.—A valley with steep sides.

Koekerboom.—A large arboreal aloe (*Aloe dichotoma*).

Kopje.—An abrupt hillock.

Mat-house.—A structure made of mats stretched over laths.

Meerkat.—A weasel-like ichneumon.

Mens.—A person.

Nachtmaal.—The celebration of the Lord's Supper.

Oom.—Uncle.

Ou' ma.—Grandmother.

Pronk.—The springbucks are said to "pronk" when they bound along with arched back and erected mane.

Ramkee.—A musical instrument resembling a banjo, which is in use among the Hottentots.

Reim.—A thong.

Sampau.—A creature resembling a tick, which is extremely poisonous.

Schepsel.—Creature, usually meant in a derogatory sense.

Scherm.—A low screen of bushes.

Tanta.—Aunt.

Trek.—(verb) To pull. The term is used to describe anything moving from place to place.

Tronk.—A prison.

Veld.—The open, uncultivated country.

Feld-kost.—Tubers, bulbs, of wild plants, suitable as food.

Chapter Seventeen.

Noquala's Cattle—A Tragedy of the Rinderpest.

A Kaffir at Home.

It was about eleven o'clock of a winter's morning in 1897 when Noquala stood before his hut and watched his cattle being driven in for milking. A noble, dun-coloured bull, in whose lowing the amatory and the defiant were about equally mingled, led the herd through the narrow gateway of the kraal, in which ample enclosure he stood, pawing the dusty manure over his shoulders and flanks. From a smaller enclosure a few yards away to the right came a chorus of agonised appeals for milk from the waiting calves. The herd of cattle numbered rather more than a hundred, and it could be seen by the most unprofessional eye that in quality its members were far superior to the usual run of cattle that one sees at the ordinary native kraal. The majority were dun-coloured.

Noquala was a jovial-looking Hlubi of about fifty years of age, stoutly built, and with a shrewd, lively eye. His hair and beard were markedly tinged with grey. His only clothing was a red blanket loosely drooped around his middle, leaving his trunk and his strong shoulders bare. On his right arm, above the elbow, he wore a thick ring of ivory; otherwise he wore no ornament whatever.

Makalipa, Noquala's wife, was sitting in the sun at the side of the hut, lazily engaged in making a mat out of rushes. She addressed her husband by name once or twice, but he, being absorbed in the contemplation of his herd of cattle, which was the thing he most loved in the world—his children not excepted—took no notice whatever of her.

"You, you—I wonder you do not sleep in the kraal; I wonder you do not eat grass," she said, in an audible soliloquy. "If I loved cattle like you do I would tie a pair of horns on my head and go on all fours.

You are more of a bull than a man, and ought to be married to a cow."

The cattle were all in by this time, and the youngest of the calves, a glossy-black little beast, was conducted to the kraal by a naked lad, about ten years of age. The little animal strained at the leash like a hound, and plunged forward with its tail twisting violently, roaring lustily the while. Others followed, and then the milking began. Noquala turned to his wife—

"What were you saying, old money-buryer?"

Makalipa was a large, spare, angular woman, whose years were probably ten less in number than those of her husband. She was dressed in a clean white skirt and a very short bodice. As the garments did not meet, a zone of black skin was strongly visible between the respective upper and nether edges. Over her head was folded, in the characteristic native fashion, a coiffure of red Turkey twill. She paused in her occupation of mat-making, letting her hands rest upon her knees, and regarded her husband with a half-angry expression.

"Have you forgotten that your son, your eldest son, Elijah, will arrive this evening, and that you promised to kill a goat so that he might have a bit of meat to eat after his long walk?"

"If you did not love your mats more than I love my cattle you would know that the best goat of my flock is now hanging in the store-hut."

"Hau! You killed it secretly, so that I might not get the skin to sell at the shop, eh?"

"Did you want the money to bury, or the meat for your son—your *eldest* son?"

Noquala walked away without giving his wife time to reply. She at once arose from her work and strode over to the store-hut, whence she emerged soon afterwards, carrying a quantity of meat, which she began to prepare for cooking.

Noquala, although a heathen, was not a polygamist—a fact, for a man of his wealth, deserving of note. Makalipa was a Christian. When he married her, twenty-two years previously, Noquala promised never to take another wife. To every one's (including, probably, Makalipa's) surprise, he never even suggested breaking his promise.

Noquala was certainly the richest man in his district. The herd of cattle which he kept at his own kraal only represented about half of his wealth. Far and wide his stock was distributed—let out to be farmed on shares, under the custom called "ngqoma," in terms of which cattle are assigned by the owner to some one who looks after them, milks them, and receives as reward a small share of the increase. Sometimes stock let out under this system is handed down from generation to generation. Even at the present day lawsuits are instituted for the recovery of cattle, the progenitors of which were assigned in the days of Tshaka. Native law recognises no prescription.

Some there were who smiled meaningly when the persistent faithfulness of Noquala to Makalipa was spoken of, and it was hinted that the rigours of his monogamy were somewhat mitigated by certain relationships which he had contracted at kraals where the whole wealth was held under his "ngqoma." Be this as it may, Makalipa seemed quite contented with her lot. She was her husband's only "wife," and that was enough for her.

Noquala was really a very liberal man, and was deservedly popular, so it was not by grasping and overreaching his fellows that he became wealthy. His success could only be attributed to sheer good fortune. His kraal was situated in a warm, fertile nook of one of the foot-ranges to the Drakensberg, and cattle throve there passing well. He inherited a fair amount of stock from his father, and this herd became a fountain of the only kind of wealth which the native values. His principle for many years had been to weed out the inferior animals, and substitute for them any superior cattle obtainable. If a young man paying "lobola" (The cattle given in payment for a wife) had a very good cow, he knew that by taking it to Noquala's kraal he could exchange it for two oxen of fair quality. As "lobola" cattle are estimated by number and not by individual value, the gain to the young man is, of course, obvious.

Goats and sheep he also had, but these he did not much regard. In fact, if it had not been for his wife he would not have had any small stock at all, except a few goats for slaughtering.

Makalipa was intensely frugal, if not miserly, by nature—and was well known to have a considerable store of money put by. She kept her wealth wrapped up in rags, and buried in various places. She had thus been amassing money by little and little for over twenty years. She claimed as her perquisite the proceeds of every skin of the respective beasts that were slaughtered or that died; and she earned a great deal by making and selling mats. The first and only time she ever drew any of her savings was when she put her son Elijah to school at Blythswood. It was her dream that Elijah should be a minister, and his own ambitions seconded hers. He was now a man of twenty-one, and had made good progress with his studies. At the point where this story opens he was expected back for his holidays. The school had broken up two days previously, and he was due to arrive within a few hours.

Noquala did not oppose actively his son's becoming educated. He would have preferred him to have followed the calling of a peasant, such as he himself was. The second son, an astute youth named Zingelagahle, was more after his father's heart. He did not care about book-learning, and was quite content to look after the cattle, knowing that the largest share of them would eventually fall to him.

The educated young native is almost invariably a prig, and cannot help showing his uncivilised relations that he feels himself to be far superior to them. As a rule this superiority is assumed by both parties; thus not much friction results.

Elijah, to do him bare justice, was perfectly sincere in his faith and in what he believed to be his vocation for the ministry. He thus felt himself to be far superior to all the others at his paternal kraal. His mother, of course, was a Christian—nominally, at least, but for years past she had taken little interest in anything but her son's education and her money-making. She did not even belong to any church. Once, when it was decided by the local Christians to erect a chapel, Noquala had been applied to for a subscription, and he had referred the applicant to his wife, stating that she had money whereas he had none. This was a literal fact. One of his peculiarities was never to own any money. Whenever taxes had to be paid or purchases had to be made, Noquala would sell to the nearest trader just sufficient sheep for the purpose, and immediately make a point of spending the last penny thus realised.

When Makalipa was applied to she had just paid her son's half-yearly fees at the seminary, and she flatly refused to contribute a sixpence towards the new building. This caused remonstrance, which was followed by recrimination. The matter ended by Makalipa withdrawing from connection with local religious enterprise. Representatives of the rival churches made advances towards this erring sheep with the heavy fleece, but without any result. Religion meant spending money, and so long, at all events, as she was paying her son's fees at the seminary she felt she was doing enough and to spare for the Kingdom of Heaven.

Chapter Eighteen.

Elijah.

It was late in the afternoon when Elijah arrived, somewhat tired from his long walk. He was a spare, loosely built youth with heavy features and a gloomy expression of countenance. His mother greeted him with much tenderness, and his father tried to be genial. But conversation between this father and son was extremely difficult. The involuntary mutual foundation of feeling was contempt, and the superstructure of conventional tolerance which formed their plane of communication was not conducive to geniality. They had thus got into the habit of having as little to say to each other as possible, and Noquala usually felt it necessary to start on one of his rounds of inspection of his "ngqoma" cattle within a few days of his son's return for the holidays.

On the present occasion the cordiality which usually was maintained between the mother and son as soon as the father's back was turned was somewhat impaired. There was a strong restraint on the son's side, which the mother found it hard to combat. When, however, Elijah had been at home for a week the cause was made clear in the following conversation:—"Mother," said Elijah, after an awkward interval, "when were you at church last?"

Makalipa flashed her keen eyes upon her son's gloomy face for an instant before she answered—

"You know quite well how it is that I do not go to church."

"Yes, mother, but I want you to go. Think what people must say about me, a man who wants to be a minister, and who has a mother who, although she is a Christian, does not go to church."

"Elijah, my son, I do not go to church, it is true, but I can read my Bible, and I don't remember the chapter in which it teaches that a son should instruct the mother who bore him. Of course, when you are a minister it will be different. Then I will go and hear you preach. So you had better make haste and have a church of your own if you want to save my soul."

Elijah walked away without replying. The day was warm, so he went and threw himself down upon his mat in the big hut in which his father and mother also slept. His mother, remorseful of having snubbed him, brought him some food a short time afterwards, but he refused to eat and said that he only wanted to sleep. Makalipa put this down to the sulks—a complaint to which Elijah had been subject to from earliest childhood—so she set the food aside and went down to the fields to superintend the harvesting of the grain.

When she returned the sun was down. Elijah was still lying on his mat, apparently asleep. His mother tried to arouse him, but he at once relapsed into a doze, after just murmuring that he had a bad headache. So Makalipa, after placing some food next to him, retired to bed and slept soundly until dawn.

When Makalipa arose she noticed that Elijah was still asleep. Something, however, in his breathing struck her as being strange. Later, when she attempted to rouse him, she found that his mind was wandering and that he was in a burning fever.

It was a severe attack of enteric fever that had struck Elijah down. A week went by, but he became worse and worse. Noquala was still away and Makalipa became more and more alarmed. At length she made up her mind to call in a European doctor, so she dug up some money and sent Zingelagahle in with it to the Magistracy, with a message asking the District Surgeon to come and visit her son.

The District Surgeon was one who had no sympathy with and therefore did not command the confidence of the natives. Not making due allowance for the limitations of the native mind, and its consequent inability to grasp the importance of attention to detail in illness, he honestly thought that in serious cases his advice, as well as the medicines he supplied, were of little avail, and he usually said so when occasion offered.

It was a long ride from the Magistracy to Noquala's kraal, and when the District Surgeon arrived the sun had nearly sunk. He meant to obtain a night's lodging at a mission station a few miles away, but he was not sure of his road and was very much afraid of being benighted. Thus he was in a great hurry to get his work over and then proceed on his journey.

Elijah had just reached the crisis of his disease when the doctor arrived. The patient was lying with nothing between him and the cold, hard floor of the hut but a rush-mat and a thin cotton blanket. He appeared to be almost at the last gasp. The doctor examined him, took his temperature, and asked as to what description of nourishment the patient had been getting. The reply he received filled him with wrath and disgust. He felt that he could do nothing, and he said so. Makalipa heard with a sinking heart that her son's hours were numbered, and that it was extremely unlikely that he would live until another sun arose. Then the doctor mounted his horse and rode away without administering any medicine, and Makalipa sat on the ground next to her son, with her heart filled with darkness, awaiting the end.

The doctor was hardly out of sight when Noquala, who had been sent for several days before, returned. He was somewhat shocked at hearing what the doctor had said, but a native never gives up hope of recovery so long as there is life in the patient. Touching Makalipa on the shoulder he beckoned to her to follow him and stepped out of the hut.

"Your European doctor has said Elijah must die, but I have seen people get better even after they have looked like that. Let us send for 'Ndakana and see what he can do."

Makalipa nodded; then she went back to the bedside of her son.

Deep down in the mind of every human being is an elementary belief in the supernatural, and when brought face to face with some terrible, incalculable danger this is apt to rise to the surface. If this be true of those who have centuries of civilisation behind them, how much more so is it in the case of those who are only struggling to emerge from barbarism? The agitated mind of Makalipa grasped greedily at the possibility which her husband's words suggested.

'Ndakana was a native "gqira," or doctor, who had made for himself a considerable reputation locally. His kraal was not more than a couple of miles distant. Thus, within an hour of being sent for, he was at the bedside of the sufferer.

The first step in his treatment was the causing of an ox to be slaughtered. The blood of this animal was sprinkled over the hut, inside and outside, the patient coming in for a share. Then with a sharpened stick he made small incisions at different parts of Elijah's body and limbs, and into these he rubbed some powder which he took from the horn of an antelope. After this he danced, violently but silently, around the hut, coming in every now and then, in a state of copious perspiration, to inquire as to how the patient was.

Soon after this Elijah was reported to be a little better. He had asked for and drunk a little sweet milk. Then 'Ndakana went home, saying that he had driven away the evil spirits, and that if the patient were kept on a milk diet for a week he would surely recover. The "gqira's" words came true. Elijah improved rapidly, and before the week was over began to complain bitterly at being allowed nothing but milk to stay his biting hunger. 'Ndakana was made happy by a fee which took the form of two of Noquala's best cattle.

Elijah was by no means grateful for the means which had been undertaken towards his recovery. That he, a Christian and a candidate for the ministry, should have been practised upon by a magician—one of a class which formed the greatest obstacle to the spread, of Christianity among the people—was a bitter reflection. Having been more or less unconscious throughout his illness, he did not know how bad he had been, and was thus firmly convinced that he would have recovered without 'Ndakana's assistance.

The mother, however, thought differently. She remembered the sinking of the heart with which she had heard the European doctor condemn her son to death, and how the patient had immediately taken a change for the better when 'Ndakana's treatment once commenced. Thus arose another cause of estrangement between mother and son.

Elijah was still weak when he decided to return to the seminary, not wishing to lose the opening of the session. His father lent him a horse for the occasion, and sent Zingelagahle on foot after him to bring the animal back.

Chapter Nineteen.

The Tempter.

An ominous whisper sounded over the land. Far to the north, it was said, a new and terrible disease had broken out among cattle. The herds of Khama, the Christian chief of the Bamangwato, had, so it was said, been swept utterly away. Like a wayward wind, it was reported, the disease swept hither and thither, leaving nothing but bleaching skeletons to mark its track. Even the wild game of the forest and the plain went down before the might of the plague. When British Bechuanaland was swept and the pestilence reached the herds of the Basuto, it was felt that the danger was indeed at the door of every owner of cattle in South Africa.

The Cape Government selected natives of reputed skill as cattle doctors, and sent them up to where the rinderpest was raging, so as to give them an opportunity of testing their remedies where the appliances of the profoundest science had failed. Upon the return of these men to their homes meetings of natives were called, and addresses embodying an account of the observed ravages of the pest were made to them. Thus the native mind became familiarised with the danger, and familiarity bred contempt. Magistrates urged upon their people the extreme danger of keeping all their wealth locked up in such a dangerously threatened item as cattle, and tried to induce them to make use of the market which existed at Johannesburg for the purpose of realising at all events a portion of their stock; but all in vain. "The 'red-water' came," they said; "we have had war, drought, lung-sickness, and other misfortunes. We will, no doubt, lose many cattle, but with what remains we will again get rich. Of what use is money to us?"

Nearer and nearer came the plague; closer and closer were drawn in the coils of that deadly chain, the links of which were flung over the desolated earth in white heaps. The demand for meat became greater and greater at Johannesburg, and agents were sent down by the different butchering firms to endeavour to purchase slaughter stock. A few sheep they managed to obtain, but no cattle.

Makalipa tried hard to persuade her husband to sell at all events some of his "ngqoma" cattle, but not a single head would he dispose of. A local trader persuaded him of what was partly true, namely—that his flock of sheep, which had increased considerably during the past few years, and of which Makalipa was joint owner, was damaging the pasturage which he required for his cattle. It was, therefore, not difficult to persuade Noquala to dispose of the sheep, which he did, much to Makalipa's dissatisfaction.

The money remained in the trader's hands, Noquala fearing to bring it home lest his wife should get hold of it. He meant to give her her share of it, but the largest portion he intended to reinvest in cattle as soon as the rinderpest danger should be at an end.

A few days later Noquala had occasion to visit the shop of another trader who lived some miles away. This man had heard of the sheep transaction and had laid his plans accordingly.

Soon after Noquala arrived a herd of cattle was driven up and shown to him. Among this herd were several most beautiful dun-coloured cows—dun being a colour in cattle which Noquala was particularly partial to. After hesitating for a few minutes he asked the trader whether the cattle were for sale or not. The trader, feigning reluctance, consented to discuss the matter. Eventually a bargain was struck. The trader, having ascertained how much of a balance lay to Noquala's credit at the other shop, drew out an order for it in his own favour, to which document Noquala affixed his mark in the presence of witnesses. Then Noquala drove home to his kraal the dun-coloured cows which, with several other cattle slightly inferior, although of fairly good quality, had now become his property.

Makalipa fell into a rage when she learnt what her husband had done. The rinderpest danger was very imminent to her, and she felt, rightly, that her husband had been guilty of stark madness in investing money in more cattle. She felt this the more keenly as the sheep had been disposed of against her strongest wishes.

"And you have even spent that portion of the money which belonged to me in buying beasts that will disappear like burning grass when the sickness comes!" she said, almost in tears.

"Whatever is the good of money to you?" he replied. "Cows have calves, but the money you bury in the earth brings nothing forth."

"The money I bury in the earth will not get the rinderpest. After the sickness has swept over the land and your kraal has been emptied, my money will still be there."

"Sickness—you are always talking about this sickness! Has not the sickness been here before, and is not my kraal still full? What does a woman know about things?"

"A woman knows more than you. Wait; on the day when your kraal stands empty my kraal will be full, and I will see you making clay oxen like a little boy, and playing with them. When your cattle all die you will go mad, if you don't die with them."

The acquisition of the new lot brought more cattle to the kraal than the enclosure could conveniently hold, so a number of the less valuable animals were weeded out and given under "ngqoma" to a man in the Xalanga district, to whom Noquala had long promised stock. This man took away five cows and five heifers to his kraal in one of the gloomy gorges of the Drakensberg.

The rinderpest came closer and closer. Its fell influence lay around the territory in which Noquala lived like a crescent, or rather like the Zulu battle-formation, which has been likened appropriately to the horns of a charging bull. But beyond a passing feeling of uneasiness when some traveller related what he had witnessed of the ravages of the pest, Noquala felt no fear. Other plagues, which had been preceded by alarming rumours, had come and gone. He, like his fellows, had suffered, although not to the same degree. He gradually made up his mind that he would, if the plague came, doubtless suffer again, but he trusted to his luck and felt sure that all would come out right in the end.

However, as the shower of rumours thickened, even Noquala began to feel uneasy. He had been told that the disease might suddenly appear, mysteriously and without apparent infection from outside. Once or twice, when individuals of his herd fell sick of minor ailments, he became distinctly alarmed. Still the rumours thickened, and his nerves began to suffer. Nevertheless he scouted every suggestion towards selling any of his cattle.

The younger children at the kraal were, as is usual with native children, in the habit of making miniature cattle out of clay. This is the sole form of plastic decorative art which the Bantu practise, with the exception of the moulding of grotesque faces on their pottery, which the Hlubis and the Basuto sometimes indulge in. The ox-moulding is of a distinctly conventional type, all the artist's attention being concentrated upon the head, horns and neck, which are often very well executed. The legs and body are usually rough and shapeless. This form of rudimentary art has probably been acquired from the Hottentots; Hottentot children who have never been in contact with the Bantu mould images of exactly the same type, and that type does not suggest the cattle kept by the Bantu at the present day, but rather those which the now nearly extinct Hottentots once owned in great numbers.

Noquala's mind often dwelt upon his wife's prophecy, and whenever he noticed the clay toys he felt a twinge of guilty uneasiness. He now knew that he had been distinctly foolish in purchasing more cattle with the proceeds of the sheep. Nevertheless he still flatly refused to sell.

Darker and ever darker grew the prospect. What was it, this disease which came like a ghost from nowhere, and slew like spears in pursuit of a beaten and exhausted foe? Lung-sickness and red-water men knew. These thinned the herds out cruelly, sometimes, but a few were always spared. But this unknown scourge that swept through the land as a fire sweeps over mountain and valley in the autumn, leaving utter desolation behind it—what could it be? Surely those who work spells of evil must be at work, or else the "imishologu" (Spirits) must be wroth on account of some great and grievous sin committed by the people.

'Ndakana, the "gqira," came into Noquala's mind. He had shown his power over evil spirits, and had driven death, vanquished, from the mat upon which his son lay. 'Ndakana professed—an unusual circumstance—to be able to heal cattle as well as men. Noquala thought he would consult with the "gqira" next time the latter came to the kraal. Pride, and a feeling that he could not bear to confess that the oft-vaunted faith in his luck had weakened, would not allow of a message being sent.

Then it was reported that the Government had found out a cure for the disease—that by injecting some mysterious and magical medicine into the blood of beasts they were rendered proof against the pest. All the same the reports of whole herds dying out like drones before the doorway of a bees' nest came over the Drakensberg from Basutoland. The mind of Noquala swayed hither and thither between the poles of confidence and despair.

One day 'Ndakana appeared at the kraal, where some beer had been brewed. The beer-drink did not degenerate into an orgie, as beer-drinks frequently do. The guests were hospitably entertained, three goats having been slaughtered for their consumption. Towards the end of the day the "gqira" drew Noquala into conversation.

"Have you never thought of having your cattle doctored?" he asked.

Noquala admitted that such an idea had occurred to him.

"I suppose you have heard of this new medicine that the Government claims to have found out," continued 'Ndakana, "and of how it has sometimes cured and sometimes failed?"

"Yes, I have heard of it."

"Well, now, I will tell you the truth about the matter. The Government found out about herds that had been treated by our doctors, and then they sent their own cattle doctors to administer medicine, so that they might claim the credit."

Noquala looked incredulous. He had had some experience of the frauds of the native doctors; when the red-water had attacked his own herd, years previously, the "gqira" he had called in promised certain cure, but the promise had miserably failed. Still, he had seen this man 'Ndakana drive death away from the bedside of his son, and that after the European doctor had confessed himself vanquished.

The sun was going down and 'Ndakana glanced keenly once or twice towards the glowing west. He strolled a few paces forward, leading his companion by, as it were, a conversational leash. When he stopped, still talking, he faced the sunset and his companion had his back to it. The "gqira's" glances, which had now become more rapid and frequent, were still directed to the pyre of the dying day.

Suddenly he lifted his hand, and his voice became vehement.

"Noquala, man of many cattle, I know the secret and I will save your herd from destruction if you will let me do so. Do you demand a sign to prove my power?"

"Show me a sign," replied Noquala, looking steadfastly into the "gqira's" eyes.

"Behold it, then."

'Ndakana took a pace forward and brushed past his companion's shoulder, at the same time flinging his hand forward with a sweep, and holding it, quivering and extended to its full length, in the direction of the sunset.

Noquala turned and looked. There, rimmed with fire, floated a cloud in the semblance of a bull stumbling forward upon one knee, in the attitude of a buffalo that has received its death wound. As he looked the gold faded out and the cloud broke up into formless wreaths of mist.

The portent struck Noquala to the heart; its short duration added to the illusion, for memory enhanced the value of every detail, and his startled imagination clothed the picture with an exactness of outline which it had never possessed.

"Doctor my cattle," he said huskily, "and you shall have great reward."

'Ndakana told his dupe that a necessary condition towards successful doctoring was that every beast possessed by the latter, whether under "ngqoma" or not, had to be brought down to the kraal by a certain date, when the state of the moon would be propitious. Noquala was now in a condition of keen excitement, and was prepared to do whatever the "gqira" might tell him. These two, the duper and the dupe, sat and talked over the matter far into the night. Makalipa insisted upon being admitted to their counsels. She, having been much impressed by the cure which she fully believed 'Ndakana to have effected in the case of her son, had no objection to offer, except upon one point. She thought it ill-advised that the last lot of cattle—those given under "ngqoma" to the man who dwelt in the Drakensberg gorge—should be brought down from a spot so near the area in which the rinderpest was raging.

But 'Ndakana insisted on the assembling of all the cattle, without any exception whatever, so she had to give in, although she did so with secret misgivings. He would, of course, give no indication whatever of the form which his doctoring was to take; that would be quite contrary to professional etiquette, and was not to be expected for a moment.

Next morning at day-dawn Noquala mounted a horse and rode around to the different kraals where his stock was to be found, warning the custodians that they were to produce every hoof and horn on the fifth day following, on pain of the "ngqoma" contract being forthwith rescinded. Zingelagahle was sent on a tough pony to the sun-forsaken gorge where the recipient of the last "ngqoma" dwelt, and which was rather a long day's ride distant, with a message to a similar effect.

In the meantime the "gqira" was busy making his preparations. A few miles away, in a shallow valley, were some extensive swamps which harboured myriads of frogs. Of the latter he collected several hundreds, which he imprisoned in wicker baskets. These he tightly secured at the openings and then sunk in the swampy water.

It is customary with the natives to keep their stores of corn in large circular excavations in the floor of the cattle enclosure. Each excavation has a narrow neck, just large enough to admit a boy of about twelve years of age who, when it is necessary to extract corn from the granary, is lowered down. The narrow mouths of these pits are closed with flat stones, and are some distance below the surface of the enclosure. Some such contain as many as half a dozen pits, the openings to which can only be located by probing through the thick dung-crust until the flat stones covering them are found.

The native doctor always keeps himself acquainted with details, no matter how apparently unimportant, regarding his neighbours—their huts, kraals, cattle, family matters, and, in fact, everything. In the case of rich and important men more attention is naturally bestowed. When called in professionally the "gqira" never likes to have to ask for any information. Divining is part of his trade, and it is thus very effective to be able to tell the dwellers of a kraal about things which they are firmly convinced nobody but themselves is aware of.

Now, as a matter of fact, 'Ndakana knew as much about Noquala's kraal and everything in it as did the Germans, when they invaded France, of the country before them. However, on the present occasion he only had occasion to use one of the many facts with which he was acquainted. He knew that one of the corn-pits in Noquala's kraal was empty, and he decided to use that pit as the base of his magical operations.

Early on the third day the troop of cattle from the Drakensberg arrived. They were in splendid condition and seemed to have improved under the change of pasturage. The enclosure formerly used for the sheep had been well bushed up, and was now available as a supplementary cattle enclosure. By the evening of the fourth day the last drove of cattle had arrived.

How Noquala feasted his eyes upon the great lowing herd! How the rival bulls, hearing each other lowing, dashed together with a shock as of mountain meeting mountain, whilst the mild-eyed cows looked on, supremely indifferent as to which should prove the victor. The owner's heart swelled with pride. All these were his—his very own, and to do what he liked with. Surely none but the great chiefs of the past had ever owned such a noble assemblage of cattle.

Many thoughts floated through the elated mind of Noquala on that June evening as he strolled through the valley with his crowd of dependents behind him at a respectful distance. He tasted the sweets of amplified possession, and drained the cup of enjoyment to the very dregs. He thought of how impossible it would have been for him, a common man, to have owned so much wealth in the old days, when the chiefs reigned supreme, and when a man who became too rich and powerful was smelt out and tortured to death. Then he thought of how lucky it was that, through the agency of the potent 'Ndakana, he was enabled to ensure these creatures that he loved and took such pride in, from harm.

At dusk the cattle were driven into the two ample enclosures, which they just comfortably filled. Some trouble was experienced in securing the different bulls, of which there were five altogether. However, these were eventually caught and tied up with strong thongs, and then Noquala and his guests retired to the big hut, where a feast of goat's flesh was laid ready.

Not so 'Ndakana. The "gqira" had more important work on hand than feasting. When night fell he hurried to the swamp where lay the baskets with the imprisoned frogs. These he now carried carefully in the direction of Noquala's kraal.

After setting down the baskets in the bottom of a dried-up donga, 'Ndakana went to a spot hard by where, behind a fringe of bushes, he had hidden away a large calabash full of water. Lifting this carefully to his shoulder, and carrying the two baskets with one hand, he made his way to the cattle enclosure. He did not want to be seen, but had he been it would not have particularly mattered, for it would only have been supposed that he was performing rites preliminary to the morrow's doctoring. However, he managed to reach the kraal and to enter it without being seen by any one and without alarming the cattle.

The "gqira" knew approximately the situation of the empty pit, so he had no difficulty in finding the flat covering stone by probing with the iron spike which he had brought with him for the purpose. Then he carefully removed the dung and opened the pit.

After making sure that the pit was really empty, and therefore the right one, 'Ndakana carefully poured into it the water from the calabash, and then emptied the frogs from the respective baskets into the narrow opening. This done, he closed the pit again and replaced the flakes of dung over the stone. The upper layer was dry and dusty, so he had no difficulty in obliterating the traces of his work. Besides, he knew that the cattle would tramp restlessly about the enclosure when it became cold towards morning, and that their feet would leave no trace of his presence visible. Then he stole away and hid in a patch of forest which grew at the head of the kloof in which Noquala's kraal is situated, and about a mile distant from the huts.

Chapter Twenty.

How the Cattle were Doctored.

Next morning the cattle were let out to graze, and again the enraptured eye of Noquala drank in delight from the contemplation of his wealth. About half an hour after sunrise the "gqira" was seen emerging with slow and stately steps from the patch of bush in which he had spent the night. Pretending not to be aware of any one else's existence, he walked straight to the cattle kraal. As soon as he entered the gate he began to stagger about wildly, and before he reached the middle he sank to the ground, apparently in a violent fit.

The people crowded round and gazed at him with awe through the upright poles forming the palisade. The fit over, he lay as though in a swoon for some considerable time, after which he sat up with a dazed expression and began groping about the enclosure on his hands and knees. When he reached the vicinity of the pit which he had opened during the previous night, he again fell over and lay quite still. By this time he was completely naked, having thrown away his blanket in the course of his progress. In his hand was the iron spike, and with this he began to dig wildly, scattering the flakes of dung far and wide.

When the stone was nearly uncovered, 'Ndakana sank back as though exhausted, and feebly called for assistance. Noquala and a number of other men at once hurried in, and he signed to them to remove the covering stone and thus open the pit. This was soon done.

'Ndakana then said that a boy must be let down into the pit, declaring that a great wonder would be revealed therein. At this all the boys who had been looking through the palisade fled away in different directions. Two or three were soon caught and dragged back, howling, to the edge of the opening. Selecting the one whose size appeared to be most suitable, the "gqira" ordered him to descend, but the boy yelled with redoubled vigour and struggled violently to escape. Then Noquala called out to one of the women to bring a rod, and with this he thrashed the unhappy youth unmercifully until the latter consented to do what was required of him. The boy, silent and wild-eyed with terror, was thereupon lowered into the dark pit through the narrow mouth.

"What do you find there?" asked the "gqira."

"I am standing in water," called the boy, his voice sounding hollow from the depths.

"Feel if there be any living thing."

"Au—there are snakes," yelled the boy, and his hands grasped the edges of the opening as he tried to draw himself up.

"They are not snakes! they are frogs," replied 'Ndakana.

At the same time Noquala cut the boy's fingers sharply with the rod. The wretched creature dropped back to the bottom of the pit with a screech of mingled pain and terror.

A basket was passed down to him, and this he was directed to fill with frogs. This, when handed up, was emptied into a larger basket, and then passed back. After several basketfuls had been taken out, the unhappy boy was assisted to come out of his prison, and the pit was closed up at once.

'Ndakana then addressed the assembled crowd. He told them that the wonder he had revealed to them was a special grace vouchsafed by the "imishologu" in response to his incantations, and that the frogs were to be utilised in doctoring Noquala's cattle so as to render them proof against the ravages of the dreaded disease.

A deep awe had fallen upon all. They felt that they were in the presence of a master wonder-worker. Noquala was now sure that his beloved cattle were safe, and his heart overflowed with gratitude to the "gqira" and to the "imishologu" who had shown such favour.

The cattle were now driven up in lots of about fifty each. When in the enclosure they were caught separately and skilfully thrown. An incision was then made in the nose of each, as well as in a frog. The reptile was then held so that its flowing blood mingled with that of the beast. As soon as this had been effected, the latter was loosened and turned out of the enclosure. A fresh cut was made in the frog for each beast treated, but as soon as the reptile died or it was found that no more blood would flow from it another frog was brought, the worn-out one being carefully put away into a basket. The frogs were thus believed to have absorbed the latent disease.

By sundown all the cattle had been treated in this manner, and then the dead frogs were thrown into a deep pit. Red-hot coals were then thrown upon them, and the pit was closed up, the earth being stamped firmly down.

But the issues at stake were too great for the caprice of the "imishologu" to be risked. More ritual must be performed on the third and fifth day, and in the meantime feasting had to take place. Otherwise the "imishologu" might, as they had often been known to do, change their shadowy, if powerful minds.

Thus, as the "gqira" pronounced it to be unsafe to remove the cattle before the sixth day, the hearts of the company were lifted up with great joy, for they knew that the exigencies of the occasion demanded that unrestricted feasting should take place during the interval.

It was here that the astute 'Ndakana made his great mistake. He should have taken his reward, which would have been, under the circumstances, a most liberal one, and removed with it to a distance. But the greatest men sometimes make mistakes, and 'Ndakana proved that he was no exception to this general rule.

Chapter Twenty One.

The Disease Appears.

The circumstance of 'Ndakana's having been so positive that the cattle would not take the rinderpest might easily puzzle those unacquainted with the methods of the native doctor, nevertheless it was quite characteristic. Although a colossal humbug, the "gqira," to a certain extent, believes in his own powers. As is the case in other walks of life, he gets so into the habit of deceiving others that he ends by deceiving himself. Probably, however, in this case 'Ndakana may have believed the reports which just about that time were current as to the Cape Government having succeeded in staying the destroying course of the disease by erecting a fence across the continent and keeping all animals away from its vicinity. Moreover the accidental resemblance to a bull which the cloud had taken may easily have been regarded by 'Ndakana's superstitious mind as a sign that the progress of the disease had been stayed. Superstition and fraud have in all ages gone hand in hand.

Again, it must be remembered that the reputation of a native doctor can only be made by taking risks. One lucky guess, one confident prophecy which happens to be crowned with fulfilment by the capricious Fates, and a "gqira" may be sent spinning dizzily along the road of success with such a momentum that many subsequent minor failures are condoned. Of course, the day comes at length when the luckiest "gqira" makes a mistake of such importance that he has to flee the neighbourhood and ever afterwards hide his diminished head. It is a well-known fact that under the rule of the native chiefs the "gqira" seldom died a natural death.

Three days of feasting took place at Noquala's kraal, the neighbours from far and near being bidden to it. Noquala was so pleased at his cattle having been rendered safe from the threatened scourge that he did not mind several of his fattest oxen being slaughtered for the occasion. Just about sundown on the third day one of the herd-boys mentioned that a certain heifer did not appear to be quite well.

Noquala heard the news without uneasiness; it was seldom that one got such a large herd of cattle together without some of them becoming afflicted with one or other of the major or minor ills that bovine flesh is heir to.

However, Noquala left the feasters and, directed by the boy, walked down the hillside to where the sick heifer was standing. It turned out to be one of the dun-coloured stock he had recently purchased out of the proceeds of the sheep, and which had been brought down from the Drakensberg.

The heifer certainly looked sick—very sick indeed. Its coat was staring; it was breathing heavily and groaning at intervals. From its nostrils was running a mass of thick, unclean, mucous discharge; water copiously ran out of its eyes; its ears hung, not downwards, as is usually the case with a sick beast, but backwards.

Noquala felt a shaft of sick dread transfix him. He stood before the poor animal, which was evidently suffering acute pain. Its muzzle retracted at each breath as one sees the nostrils of a human being retract in severe cases of asthma. The creature turned an appealing eye upon him—a large, beautiful dark eye, to which agony had lent a strange and pathetic intelligence. Noquala's eyes grew moist, and a spasm contracted his throat. He suffered with the suffering of the thing that he loved.

While he was regarding the sick heifer Noquala heard the sound of approaching footsteps, so after hastily getting rid of any signs of emotion, he turned to meet the comer. This turned out to be a native policeman, who, executing some message from the magistrate of the district, had sniffed the feast from afar and turned aside to partake in it. After he had carefully examined the heifer the policeman returned to where he had left his horse. Then he informed the company that he had suddenly remembered something which made it impossible for him to spend the night, as he had already expressed his intention of doing, with the feasters. After this he rode away in the direction of the Magistracy.

Next morning the Magistrate was awakened out of his slumbers by word that a policeman wanted to see him upon important business. The police had been carefully warned to examine into and report upon suspicious cases of bovine disease which might come under their notice. At the same time the superficial symptoms of rinderpest were explained to the men so that they might better be able to diagnose cases of illness coming under their personal notice.

In the present instance the symptoms reported by the constable suggested rinderpest so exactly that the Magistrate immediately mounted his horse and rode to Noquala's kraal so as personally to investigate matters. He was accompanied by four mounted constables for use in the event of the worst contingency being realised.

Noquala, after contemplating the sufferings of the sick heifer, had no stomach for the feast. However, darkness had fallen, so nothing more could be done until the following day. At earliest dawn he was among his cattle. The dun-coloured heifer was evidently dying. It was lying down where he had left it on the previous night, with its head turned back against its shoulder—an attitude which Noquala had never previously noticed in the case of a sick beast. Its extremities were cold, its nostrils were inflamed. The soft, suffering glance from the mild brown eye beamed out through a ring of foul, caked mucus, and struck a chill into the gazer's soul.

He went with hurried steps to the large cattle-fold. Three other animals struck him as looking seedy. What he particularly noticed was the peculiar backward droop of the ears and the copious running from the eyes and nostrils. He opened the gate and drove out the whole herd. Then he called the boys and also the man from the Drakensberg, and had the cattle which had come from there driven back into the enclosure.

The examination did not diminish his uneasiness. Seven animals appeared to be sick. Every minute the symptoms appeared to increase with horrible rapidity. 'Ndakana was sent for, and arrived drowsy with repletion. He made light of the affair, saying that the animals were probably seedy from a change of pasturage—a thing which often happened when cattle were brought down from the mountains to the low country.

The Drakensberg cattle were herded together during the day, by afternoon they were all sick. The heifer was still lingering in agony, but evidently its hours were numbered. Noquala wandered from one suffering creature to another, his heart rent with their pangs and his soul quaking with fear.

Just before sundown the Magistrate arrived and made an examination. There was, he said, no doubt that the disease was the dreaded rinderpest. He drew a cordon around the valley in which Noquala's kraal was situated, and put a chain of guards to see that no animal left the infected area.

Noquala and 'Ndakana had a long and serious conversation, the result of which was that the former's fears were somewhat stilled. What did the Magistrate know of cattle? asked the "gqira." The beasts were all right. Those from the Drakensberg had apparently eaten of some poisonous herb on the way down. A few might die, but the others would recover. He—'Ndakana—would stake his reputation on the correctness of his view. In the meantime he would go to the bush and dig out some roots which were an infallible remedy against the results of eating poisonous bushes.

The infallible remedy was administered, but it had small, if any, effect. Next day the heifer was dead, and every one of the Drakensberg cattle appeared to be doomed. Then they began to die, one by one at first; afterwards by twos and threes. Some appeared to take a turn towards recovery, only suddenly to succumb. The "gqira" was voluble over the effects of the poison. He remembered just such a similar case taking place in the Hlangweni country, where he had once lived. None of the other cattle showed signs of sickness as yet, so Noquala fully accepted the poison-bush theory.

But it could be seen that the "gqira" was uneasy. Every morning he would turn out before any one else, and spend a long time among the cattle. Then, when the others rose from their slumbers, he would triumphantly report that there was no sign of disease among any but the Drakensberg herd. One morning, however, he failed to make his triumphant report; in fact, when the others arose, there was nothing of the "gqira" to be seen. One of the boys said that he had been entrusted with a message from 'Ndakana to the effect that the latter had gone to a more distant forest to get some roots of greater potency than any obtainable close at hand.

Noquala went down to the kraal, and noticed that a number of cattle, besides those of the Drakensberg herd, were showing signs of sickness.

From that morning the kraal of Noquala knew the presence of 'Ndakana the "gqira" no more.

When the sun went down that day every member of the Drakensberg herd was dead, and a number of other cattle were sick with symptoms similar to those they had suffered from.

Chapter Twenty Two.

The Tragedy.

The agony of Noquala now entered into its acute stage. The guards were posted around the vale of pestilence and mourning in a pitiless ring. Dozens of men were at work inside with pick and spade, digging pits for the interment of the carcases. Soon, however, the deaths became so many that the diggers could not keep pace with them, so the carcases were allowed to lie and rot in the sunshine. Later, as the animals fell sick, they were driven up towards the head of the valley, where the stench of the dead poisoned their dying breath, and thus added another pang to those the miserable creatures already suffered from. This cruelty was rendered necessary by the circumstances of the case. It was, above all, important to confine the infection within bounds, until the surrounding herds had been inoculated.

Day by day, hour by hour, the mournful processions would wend, with the slowness of a funeral, to this ghastly spot, where the swollen carcases festered over the ground. Sometimes a doomed brute being goaded along would suddenly take fright at the stench, and, gathering a flicker of strength from its dismay, rush frantically backwards, until it tumbled in a heap to the ground. Foul carrion-birds roosted upon every stump and stone; others, gorged so that they could not fly, would hop ungainly away when disturbed, and fall into a sick sleep when they stopped at a few yards' distance.

The effluvium became so bad that it was found impossible to approach this bovine Golgotha except when the wind was favourable. When the breeze blew down the valley towards the kraal, the dwellers would be seized with violent sickness.

Noquala, who had become quite prostrated when he found that the pest had attacked his main herd and that 'Ndakana had bolted, soon recovered his self-command, and bore himself with pathetic dignity.

His hair and beard became rapidly greyer; his face grew drawn and haggard; his eyes took on the look of agony which he read, all day long, in the eyes of the beasts he loved so well, and the sufferings of which seemed to be mirrored in his consciousness. Some few—about a tenth of the herd—as yet showed no sign of infection. The noble, dun-coloured bull still stalked about majestically, breathing love and defiance in his low. Well, thought Noquala, surely all his cattle would not die; he would be left with a few with which to begin again with. Just the dun-coloured bull and a few cows. It would be a joy once more to build up wealth. No one ever heard of such a thing as that a multitude of cattle, such as his, should die out of any disease. Alas! no one with whom Noquala had foregathered had ever heard an adequate account of the fell effects of the rinderpest.

But day by day the agony deepened, until at length the time came when the splendid herd of a couple of weeks back all had expired except a few sick and staggering creatures, the superior vitality of which had prolonged for them the agonies of inevitable death. The dun-coloured bull was one of the last to succumb, but he too vailed his lordly crest and sank his deep voice to a pitch as pitiful as that of the two-year-old heifer, his dying daughter, that lay moaning close to him. The guards came to drive the last survivors to the dreadful spot at the head of the valley, but Noquala seized his sticks and rushed at them so fiercely that they fled from before his face. Then Noquala mounted guard over the last dying remnants of his matchless herd, and none dared further to disturb their agonies.

The sun went down and the pitiless stars gazed impassively on the valley of the shadow of death. Noquala remained at his post. Every now and then would he pass from one to the other of the suffering creatures, endeavouring distractedly to comfort them with words. The night was bitterly cold; a white frost thickly covered the grass and struck to the marrow of the tortured limbs. At the sharp pinch which came just before dawn, tardy Death finished his work. One by one, within a few fatal minutes, the remainder of Noquala's cattle expired. The dun-coloured bull was the last to die. He lingered until a pallid flicker filled the east. Then he started as if about to rise. For an instant it seemed as though he would succeed, for he lifted his gaunt trunk upon his front legs, and swept a dazed and startled gaze from one to the other of the carcases of his dead companions which lay around him. But he could get no farther; his hind quarters were paralysed. He remained thus for a few seconds, then, with a roar that seemed to shake the hills, he sank back and died.

Noquala was found at daybreak sitting on the ground close to the carcase of the bull. His head lay forward upon his bent knees; his grey hair was whitened by the frost. He was so stiff from the cold that he was unable to move, so had to be carried back to his hut, where they covered him with blankets and gave him a draught of hot broth, which he drank mechanically. It was long before he regained normal warmth.

When next Noquala emerged from the hut into the sunlight he was a cripple. His lower limbs had become cramped and contracted, and it was found impossible to straighten them. His memory was asleep, and it is not likely that it will ever waken. One day, as he sat in the sunshine, a little boy came up and began to play with some clay oxen, close to him. A bright smile at once lit up Noquala's face; he stretched forth his hand, seized a couple of the images, and began to fondle them.

He is, apparently, quite happy. Makalipa tends him devotedly, and helps him to hobble back to the hearth when the sun goes down or a cold wind springs up, first assisting him to gather up the clay oxen and place them carefully in a fold of his blanket. She has not the least objection to digging up her hoards, as occasions arise, and spending the money freely upon her husband's comfort. Elijah is still at the seminary, and has not yet heard of what has happened at his home.

The children of the neighbourhood take a pleasure in making clay oxen for the one-time proud, masterful, and wealthy man who has become their playmate and companion; they even make expeditions to distant valleys for the purpose of obtaining various-hued ochres and earths, so as to manufacture cattle of different colours. Noquala has now quite a large number of these toys. His only trouble is when one breaks by accident, but as they are strongly made and afterwards baked in an old ant-heap which does duty for a kiln, this does not very often occur. He seldom speaks, except when he sees a stranger approaching. Then he says, in a high, thin voice, quite different to his former gruff, deep-chested tones—

"Have you seen 'Ndakana?... He is a great doctor... He went to the bush for roots... I wonder why he does not come."

The End.